W9-CEO-575

Between the Lines

Also by the Author

Lottie's Courage: A Contraband Slave's Story

Ten-year-old Lottie is sold away from her mother at a slave auction in Williamsburg, Virginia. Bought by the evil slave trader Nephus Slye, Lottie travels south tied to other slaves. The uncertainty of her future leads Lottie to attempt escape. With Weza, an older woman who befriends her, Lottie slips away in the darkness. Morning finds the slave trader and his dogs closing in.

ISBN 978-1-57249-311-7 • Softcover

Divided Loyalties: A Revolutionary War Fifer's Story

The Revolutionary War has torn apart eleven-year-old Teddy's family. His father is a Patriot, his mother a Loyalist. Teddy mistakenly joins the wrong unit of the local regiment and enters a whole new world of men and boys headed off to war in faraway South Carolina. As a member of the fifes and drums, Teddy forges new loyalties and faces defeat at the Battle of Camden in August 1780.

ISBN 978-1-57249-369-8 • Softcover

Anybody's Hero: The Battle of Old Men and Young Boys

Luca, twelve years old and new in Civil War Petersburg, wants to fit in. No one, except Jim, the class brain, is friendly. Luca and Jim team up to investigate the mysteries surrounding the doll with no face, the Voodoo pouch, and the Trapezium House. They decide to share their suspicions with Luca's grandfather on the day the Union army advances on Petersburg. Luca, his grandfather, and Jim join the old men and young boys defending the city.

ISBN 978-1-57249-343-8 • Softcover

Lili's Gift: A Civil War Healer's Story

Based on historical records and present-day research on the little understood phenomenon of healing, Lili's Gift encompasses the plight of Civil War seamstresses in Philadelphia; the Battle of the Wilderness where more than 3,000 Union soldiers were missing; Pennsylvania orphanages for the children of Civil war soldiers; the siege of Petersburg; and the accounts of Clara Barton's "flying hospital."

ISBN 978-1-57249-392-6 • Softcover

Between the Lines

A Revolutionary War Slave's Journey to Freedom

Phyllis Hall Haislip

WHITE MANE KIDS
SHIPPENSBURG, PENNSYLVANIA

Copyright © 2012 by Phyllis Hall Haislip

ALL RIGHTS RESERVED—No part of this book may be reproduced in any form without permission in writing from the publisher, except by a reviewer who wishes to quote brief passages in connection with a review.

This book is a work of historical fiction. Names, characters, places, and incidents are products of the author's imagination and are based on actual events.

The acid-free paper used in this book meets the guidelines for permanence and durability of the Committee on Production Guidelines for Book Longevity of the Council on Library Resources.

For a complete list of available publications
please write
White Mane Kids
Division of White Mane Publishing Company, Inc.
P.O. Box 708
Shippensburg, PA 17257-0708 USA
Our catalog is also available online www.whitemane.com

Library of Congress Cataloging-in-Publication Data

Haislip, Phyllis Hall.
    Between the lines : a Revolutionary War slave's journey to freedom / Phyllis Hall Haislip.
        p. cm.
    Summary: "Twelve-year-old Cassie, a mixed-race slave, is caught between the lines in 18th century Revolutionary War Virginia"--Provided by publisher.
    ISBN 978-1-57249-409-1 (pbk. : alk. paper)
    [1. Slavery--Fiction. 2. Virginia--History--Revolution, 1775-1783--Fiction.
3. United States--History--Revolution, 1775-1783--Fiction.
4. Racially mixed people--Fiction. 5. Fugitive slaves--Fiction.] I. Title.
    PZ7.H128173Bet 2012
    [Fic]--dc23
                                                            2012003431

PRINTED IN THE UNITED STATES OF AMERICA

To my friends: Noreen Bernstein,
Janice Dixon and Viky Pedigo
who have tirelessly fostered
a love of reading in children.

Contents

Chapter 25   Richmond 109

Chapter 26   Punch and Joan 114

Chapter 27   Learning Puppetry 118

Chapter 28   Trial in Annapolis 122

Chapter 29   Philadelphia 128

Chapter 30   Snowstorm.. 131

Chapter 31   Into the Snow 135

Chapter 32   Amos Heckel 138

Chapter 33   Widow Bright 142

Chapter 34   Charles Goodfellow 148

Chapter 35   Manda and Anthony... 152

Chapter 36   At the Theater Royal 159

Author's Note 164

Educational Resources

    Glossary 167

    Lesson Plans 172

    To Plan a Visit 177

    Resources 178

Acknowledgments

My special thanks to British military reenactors encamped in Williamsburg. They graciously consented to being photographed for this book.

I am also indebted to Tab Broyles of the Colonial Williamsburg Foundation who alerted me to the goldmine that is Bowles and Carver, *Old English Cuts and Illustrations for Artists and Craftspeople.*

My thanks to Marianne Zinn, Angela Guyer, and the other hard-working staff at White Mane Kids whose attention to detail has made this a better book.

As always, I'm grateful for the support, technical help, and input of my husband, Otis Haislip.

Cassie's Journey

NY

PA

NJ

New York City

Princeton

Philadelphia

MD

Annapolis

VA

Richmond

Williamsburg

Yorktown

Map courtesy of Otis L. Haislip, Jr.

1

The Visitor

Williamsburg, Virginia 1781
Fifth year of the War of Independence

"Cassie, Massa wants you in the shop, right now. Take off that soiled apron and tuck in your hair."

Cassie dropped her scrub rag into the pail, searching Aunt Ida's dark, weathered face, so dear, yet so different from her own light skin. "What does he want me for? He never pays me no m-mind."

"I don't know, child, but someone is with him. Go on now. You'll find out soon enough what he wants."

Taking off her checked apron and handing it to Aunt Ida, Cassie tucked her springy curls under her mobcap. She cautiously made her way around mud puddles from recent spring rains to the oyster shell path that led to the Nicholses' gunsmith shop. A green and yellow coach stood in front of the shop. A coachman in green livery was

Coach and team on
Duke of Gloucester Street,
Colonial Williamsburg

Author Photograph

Gun shop interior, Colonial Williamsburg

Author Photograph

talking softly to one of the four powerful, black carriage horses stomping and snorting restlessly at the hitching post.

Cassie hesitated at the door, not wanting to go in. She had heard enough horrible slave stories to fear any change in the normal routine. A white girl, who didn't look that different from her, skipped up the street, rolling a wooden hoop. Cassie took a deep breath, stood a little straighter, and knocked on the door.

"Come in," said Mr. Nichols, her owner.

Mr. Nichols was sitting at his work table, which was cluttered with gun parts. Cassie breathed in the familiar smell of wood and gun oil. A short, stout man in a white wig with pouches under his eyes sat in the straight-back chair beside the work table, holding a cocked hat in his hand.

Mr. Nichols peered at Cassie over the glasses that rested on his long, thin nose and then turned to his guest. "Mr. Blanton, this is our Cassie. Step forward, Cassie, so Mr. Blanton can get a look at you."

Cassie edged closer to the two men, suddenly conscious her hands were chapped and her nails were ragged from scrubbing the porch. She pressed her hands closer to her rough, woolen petticoat and glanced at Mr. Blanton. In contrast to Mr. Nichols' linen shirt and cotton breeches, the visitor wore a suit with an embroidered waistcoat, silk stockings, and shoes with silver buckles.

"You say she's twelve years old." Mr. Blanton pursed his lips as if this whole business was distasteful. "Does she have any learning?"

The visitor was treating Cassie like an object by talking about her instead of to her. Mr. Nichols had told Cassie never to lower her eyes when he spoke to her. Now however, she lowered her eyes.

"She can read a few words and figure some. And . . . ," Mr. Nichols hesitated, "she stutters a little. Not bad, she has trouble getting words out sometimes. But she works hard and gives no trouble."

"No one told me the girl was tongue-tied. Are you tongue-tied, girl?"

Cassie's face grew hot as if she were leaning over the spit in the kitchen fireplace. With a great effort, she forced out the words without looking up, "Sometimes sir."

Mr. Blanton didn't say anything for a minute, probably evaluating this new information. "Could she take off her mobcap?" he asked.

Cassie reached up and took off the neat, white cap. One of her unruly auburn curls fell forward across her left eye, and she swept it back with her hand.

"With fair skin and that hair, someday she'll be a likely wench," Mr. Blanton said.

A shiver ran down Cassie's spine. She glanced up to see the visitor nod to Mr. Nichols.

"That's fine, Cassie," Mr. Nichols said. "You may go."

Cassie turned and shut the shop door quietly behind her. Then she fled, looking for Aunt Ida.

Aunt Ida sat by the table in the kitchen. Her gnarled hands, normally never still, lay in her lap. The smells of roasting pork and fresh-baked bread filled the room. She looked up with a sad smile. With her stocky build, she had always seemed to Cassie like the big oak behind the Nicholses' house—old, yet strong and enduring. However, since Mr. Blanton's visit, Aunt Ida seemed suddenly to have grown older.

"Who is Mr. B-B-Blanton?" Cassie asked anxiously. "And what does he want with me?"

"Blanton's a big landowner. There's no telling what's going on, but when white folks pay attention to you, there's always trouble."

Cassie struggled to quiet the fearful possibilities that filled her mind. The old woman rose from her chair as if going to the stocks outside the courthouse for punishment. "You need to pick greens for dinner," she said. "It'll be dinnertime before we know it."

No matter what happened, there were always chores for Cassie to do. Cassie thought about the white girl she had seen with the hoop, wondering what it would be like to have the freedom to play in the street. She put on her apron again, picked up a knife, and headed to the kitchen garden.

The Nicholses' dinner was ready in the late afternoon. Cassie removed the sizzling pork roast from its spit, put it on a platter, and took it to the dining room with its blue-figured wallpaper and mahogany table. Mr. Nichols sat at the head of the table and Mrs. Nichols at the far end. For dinner, he had put on a jacket and tied back his gray hair with a black ribbon.

Cassie next brought the steaming dish of greens to the dining room. Mr. Nichols seemed unusually intent on carving the roast.

"Just put them on the table," Mrs. Nichols said without looking at her.

As the dinner progressed, Mr. and Mrs. Nichols hardly said a word to each other whenever Cassie was in the room. Her uneasiness grew.

Cassie was clearing away dessert dishes when Mr. Nichols rose from the table. "Tell Aunt Ida, I'd like to see her in the shop," he said.

In the warm kitchen, Aunt Ida was washing the dinner dishes in a basin of soapy water. "M-Massa wants to see you in the shop," Cassie said. "I'll see to the dishes."

Aunt Ida gave her a weak smile. "That's a good girl. You've always been a good girl."

The drawn look on Aunt Ida's face told Cassie the old woman sensed something was going to happen, and it wouldn't be good. Her heart began to pound. She remembered seeing a baby bird that had fallen out of its nest, fear shaking its fragile body as it tried to scurry to the protection of tall grass. Now she wanted to run and hide too. She wished she was little enough to crawl into the bottom of the storage cupboard in the kitchen.

Instead, Cassie put her chapped hands into the hot, soapy water and washed the dishes. She was putting pots and pans on their hooks when Aunt Ida returned. One look at her tear-filled eyes told Cassie something was terribly wrong.

"I'm almost done here," Cassie said. "You go on. I'll b-be right along."

The old woman wiped her eyes with her hand and wobbled unsteadily out of the kitchen. Cassie threw out the dishwater, wiped the kitchen table, and hung the drying linens over the back of a chair. With a quick look around to make sure everything was neatly put away, she headed to the quarters she shared with Aunt Ida and Ida's husband Moses.

Their quarters were in the small clapboard cottage behind the gunsmith's shop. In the darkness, the light from the windows looked warm and inviting. Cassie found the old couple sitting in front of the fireplace. Moses was smoking his clay pipe while Aunt Ida stared into the fire with a handkerchief clutched in her hand.

"Have this chair, Cassie." Moses picked up a chair with one hand and placed it between them. In spite of his grizzled hair, bent back, and leathery skin, Moses had powerful arms, and he moved the chair as easily as if it were one of the creamware tea-cups on the shelf near the table.

He rose, coughing. "The fire needs more wood," he said, tapping his pipe on the inside of the fireplace. A cascade of half-burned tobacco, like falling stars, dropped down into the fire.

Cassie slipped into the chair, took off her shoes, and placed her tired feet on the hearth. She waited for Aunt Ida to say something. Finally, Cassie could wait no longer. She blurted out, "Tell m-me, Auntie, what's going on?"

Aunt Ida took a deep breath. Her eyes filled with tears that spilled down her dark face. She blew her nose in her handkerchief. "Massa tol' me he traded you to that Mr. Blanton for a boy."

2
The Last Night

"What?" Cassie couldn't believe what she had just heard. She wanted to ask Aunt Ida to explain. She opened her mouth but no words came. It was as if she had a ball of cotton in her mouth.

Aunt Ida spoke slowly, trying to recall exactly what Mr. Nichols had told her. "Massa needs a boy to help in the smithy. He tol' me General Washington hisself has placed an order for guns. And, the Continental army's sending him lots of guns to repair." Aunt Ida paused a moment before continuing. "I was glad when that no-good apprentice left to join the army. I never imagined Massa couldn't find another."

Cassie found her voice. "I've been traded I-like a horse or a heifer?" Tears sprung to her eyes and rolled down her cheeks. "I've always I-lived here. You're my family. Who'll help you with cooking and cleaning and M-Moses with the garden?"

Aunt Ida dabbed at her eyes. "We don't know how we'll get along without you."

"What will I be doing at the new place?" Cassie still was finding it very hard to speak.

"The Blantons have a little girl. You'll be looking after her and helping out in the house."

"Where do the B-B-Blantons I-live?"

"Massa tol' me it's one of those plantations along the York River between here and Yorktown. Massa say Mr. Blanton's in

7

town from time to time, meeting with the other big landowners at the Raleigh Tavern. So it can't be too far."

"Oh, Aunt Ida, I d-don't want to go away. Anywhere that isn't here is too far." Cassie tried to control the sobs that shook her. "There m-must b-be a m-mistake."

A look at Aunt Ida's sorrowful face told Cassie there was no mistake. Aunt Ida opened her arms. "Come here, child. It could be worse. You could be put on the auction block and sold south. You'll be a house servant. That's always better than working in the fields."

Cassie sat on Aunt Ida's ample lap just as she had when she was a little girl and put her arms around the dear old lady. Tears ran down Cassie's face. "I don't want to go away. I don't want to l-leave you and M-Moses."

"There, there," crooned Aunt Ida. "We have to accept the things we can't change. But there's one thing that will never change: our love for you. It'll go with you always and forever."

Moses came in with his arms full of wood. He put logs on the fire and adjusted them with the poker. Then he sat and re-trieved his pipe. He put new tobacco in the pipe, tamped it down with the flat end of a horseshoe nail, and lit it with a twig from the fire.

The combination of Aunt Ida's reassurances and Moses' ev-eryday action soothed Cassie.

"How long before I'll be going away?" she asked.

"Massa says Mr. Blanton's overseer, a Mr. Elijah Horn, will come for you tomorrow morning," Aunt Ida said.

"Tomorrow!" Cassie struggled not to break into tears again.

Moses' pipe went out. He lit it again and cleared his throat. "I've seen that fellow Horn around town. He's a mean-looking cuss. But Cassie, you'll have little to do with him, you being in the house and all."

Tears spilled out of Cassie's eyes. Aunt Ida handed Cassie a clean handkerchief and she blew her nose. She had heard about overseers from other slaves, and what she had heard wasn't good. She would have to be careful to avoid trouble.

"There's no telling what her new owner will be like." Aunt Ida shook her head sadly. Big tears rolled down her face.

It was Cassie's turn to reassure Aunt Ida. "I'll be all right," she said, trying to sound confident.

Aunt Ida wiped her eyes with her handkerchief. Moses looked for a long moment at his wife. "I know you've been putting it off, but it's time she knew about her parents," he said.

Ida shook her head. "I don't know where to begin."

"What haven't you told me? I keep l-looking for my father, hoping he'll come around the l-lilac bush at the side of the shop, whistling. But you never seem to want to talk about him," Cassie said.

"I'll begin," Moses said. "Your mother Eliza was a fine-looking woman with golden-brown skin and deep-set eyes like yours."

He paused as if he didn't know what to say next, and Aunt Ida picked up where he left off. "Eliza lived with us. She hadn't been here long when Massa decided to enlarge the gun shop. He hired Charles, your father, a very good bricklayer, to do the work."

"I don't understand. My father was a slave," Cassie said.

"He was a slave, but he had a trade. His owner hired him out and took most of his wages. Charles kept a part of what he earned, and he was saving to buy his freedom. When your mama and daddy met, it was love at first sight, and Massa gave permission for Eliza to marry."

"They were a handsome couple. No wonder you aren't half bad looking yourself," Moses interjected, puffing thoughtfully on his pipe.

Cassie knew that her mother had died in childbirth. "I guess I ruined it all when I was b-born."

Aunt Ida frowned. "Don't you blame yourself. Your daddy was crazy with grief, but he loved you dearly. You have his light skin, but you've always favored your mother right much. He spent whatever free time he could manage with you, but bitterness festered in him. He always thought that if he could have afforded a doctor instead of the midwife sent by the Nicholses, your mother might not have died."

No one said anything for a moment. "Is that all?" Cassie asked.

"Your father's situation became complicated when the Colonists rebelled against England and the War of Independence was about to start," Moses said.

"I know about the war," Cassie said, thinking about the Continental soldiers she'd often seen in town.

"But what you don't know," Moses said, "is that when you were about five, the Royal Governor, Lord Dunmore, offered freedom to all the slaves who joined the British cause. Your father, who was used to a lot of independence anyway, ran away and joined the British army in 1775."

Cassie's thoughts were in turmoil. She had heard much discussion of rights and liberties and she understood that the Patriots favored both. It was confusing that her father had gained his freedom from slavery by joining the British. "But the B-British are fighting to prevent the Colonists from gaining their freedom."

"The British offered slaves freedom only to plague the Patriots," Moses said. "If a whole lot of slaves ran off, the planters would have no one to hoe tobacco. And tobacco puts sterling into the pockets of the Patriots. Sterling that they could use to fight the war."

"Why didn't you tell me this b-before?" Cassie asked, trying to keep anger out of her voice. "Didn't you trust me?"

"Probably I should've tol' you, but I kept putting it off. I had my reasons," Aunt Ida said.

Cassie pictured her powerfully built father wearing the red coat and white breeches of a British soldier. He would be carrying a gun. Perhaps he would even ride a horse. He could protect her from the uncertain future with her new owners.

"M-Maybe I can join the B-British, too. Why do we have to accept the things we can't change? My father didn't accept things."

"But he's a grown man, not a young girl." Moses reached over and awkwardly patted her with his gnarled hand. "A young girl by herself can't go running off to the British, no matter how many proclamations they issue, no matter how many promises they make to slaves who run away. Besides, the British want soldiers, not youngsters."

In spite of Moses' warning words, Cassie could see herself already with the British army. They would surely recognize she was courageous and hardworking and want her to stay.

"M-Maybe if I could m-manage to reach the B-British, m-maybe I'd find my father. M-Maybe then no one could trade me away from those I l-love."

"Don't go getting any foolish ideas." Aunt Ida shook a finger at Cassie. "I doubt your father's anywhere hereabout or we'd have heard from him. Remember, he's an escaped slave, and some people would call him a traitor too."

The image of her father as a powerful soldier had not faded from Cassie's mind. For the first time, since she had heard the terrible news she was leaving her home, she found a reason for hope. "B-But I'll have no one without you. No one, but Father. I m-may never be able to return to Williamsburg, and you, but m-maybe I can find him."

Tears welled in Aunt Ida's eyes and Moses sadly shook his head. The three of them sat quietly before the fire. As the minutes passed, Cassie didn't want the evening ever to be over. She guessed Aunt Ida and Moses felt the same. The quarters grew colder as Cassie watched the coals in the fire wink out one by one.

A last log burned down to ashes and Aunt Ida seemed to draw herself together. "Cassie, you go along to bed. Tomorrow will be here before we know it."

Cassie hugged the old couple and then, half-blinded with tears, climbed the ladder into the loft where she slept. Her brave thoughts of escape to the British vanished as she thought of the coming separation from Aunt Ida and Moses. She had long known because they were old she couldn't live with them forever. But she hadn't guessed she would be parted from them so soon. She wasn't sure she could survive without them. Tears flooded her eyes again as she fumbled to take off her petticoat, shoes, and stockings. She was climbing under the patchwork quilt in her shift when she heard Moses whisper, "Ida, is that all you are going to tell her?"

Cassie strained to hear Aunt Ida's hushed voice. "She knows everything she needs to know. What she doesn't know can't hurt her."

3
Leaving Home

Morning came and Cassie rose and began to dress. Her eyes smarted from last night's tears and her heart felt as heavy as a millstone. She smelled bacon Aunt Ida was cooking in the large skillet in the fireplace as she gathered her clothes and put them into a tow sack.

Moments later, Cassie joined the old couple at the worn plank table where she had eaten so many meals. Aunt Ida served her a steaming plate of potatoes and bacon. "Eat up," Aunt Ida said. "You'll need your strength."

Cassie ate a piece of bacon and it seemed to settle into a lump in her stomach. She put down her fork.

Aunt Ida rose and opened the chest where she stored clothes and an extra quilt. From the bottom, she drew out a woman's short jacket. The jacket, made of printed beige cotton on which red-and-green flowers formed an elegant pattern, was laced up the front and lined with linen. "This belonged to your mama. Massa gave her a fine piece of cotton one Christmas and she made the jacket, copied the pattern from one she'd seen in the millinery shop. She wore it with a nice black petticoat the day she and your father were married. It'll almost fit you. She wanted me to save it for you. It's best you take it with you."

Aunt Ida handed Cassie the jacket. Cassie took it and turned it over in her hands, admiring the skillful handwork. She held the jacket to her face for a moment. It smelled of lavender. She had never owned anything that had belonged to her mother. "Thank you, for keeping it for m-me, Aunt Ida." She put it into her tow sack.

Moses removed a floor board and took out a little bag. He handed Cassie two shillings. "I want you to have these, to remember us by."

"Remember you?" Cassie's voice broke. "How could I ever forget the two d-dearest people I've ever known?"

Moses held out the coins. Cassie hesitated. British money was scarce and the shillings were valuable and she was unwilling to take half of their small savings. "You may need them," Aunt Ida said. "There's no telling what the future will bring."

Cassie took the shillings, sniffling to keep from crying. Aunt Ida tore a strip of rag and handed it to Cassie. "Tie those coins up in this rag and put them in your extra pair of stockings." Cassie tied up the coins in the rag and put them into her sack.

"Don't you go and break down now," Aunt Ida warned. "Have a cup of tea."

Aunt Ida poured them all a cup of mint tea. Cassie had just about finished hers when there was a loud rap on the door. It sent chills down her spine.

When neither Aunt Ida nor Moses moved, Cassie went to the door. A short, muscular man with a receding hairline and a pock-marked face stood in the doorway. He held a sweat-stained slouch hat in his hand. He was without a doubt Mr. Blanton's overseer, Mr. Horn. "You must be the girl," he said. "Come along."

Putting on the navy coat that had once belonged to the Nicholses' daughter, Cassie picked up the tow sack. She was about to hug Aunt Ida and Moses one last time when Mr. Horn roughly grabbed Cassie's arm and pulled her away. "Hurry along," he ordered. "I don't have all day."

Cassie's eyes filled with tears. As they headed to the wagon, she glimpsed the new boy standing by the back door to the house. He was tall and skinny and probably a year or two older than she was. Mr. Nichols was speaking with him and the boy looked uncomfortable. Cassie knew how he felt.

Mr. Horn's fingers bit into her arm as she turned to look at Aunt Ida and Moses one last time. They stood forlornly in the doorway. "Everything will be all right!" Moses called out to her.

The pale morning sun peeked in and out of heavy, gray clouds. Cassie shivered, feeling as desolate as the bleak March day, as she rode beside Mr. Horn on the high, hard seat of the farm wagon. The only sounds were the creaking of the wheels on the rutted road and the rumbling of the two hogsheads of molasses in the back of the wagon. She dried her tears, but she was still crying on the inside.

As the wagon lumbered along, the overseer lit his pipe. The familiar smell of tobacco brought Moses' last words to mind. Cassie took a deep breath, hoping that everything would not be as bad as she feared.

They had been on the road for about a half hour when they rounded a curve and she saw an imposing three-story, brick mansion. The Governor's Mansion in Williamsburg was the biggest building Cassie had ever seen, and this house rivaled it in size and in grandeur.

"Blanton Hall," Mr. Horn grunted, pointing his whip in the direction of the house. He entered the circular driveway and stopped before an impressive door with a brass doorknocker. Cassie must have been gaping because Mr. Horn explained in a gruff voice, "This is the back of the house. The front faces the river."

Before they could alight, a black man in dark green livery faced with yellow opened the door. "Good mornin', Mr. Horn," he said.

The overseer indicated to Cassie with a jerk of his head that she should get down. She stood and the doorman offered her his hand, helping her down from the wagon. "You must be Zinnia's new gal. I'll take you to her," he said.

Mr. Horn clucked to the horses and the wagon disappeared around the corner of the building. Cassie's legs shook as she followed the doorman up the steep steps and through the massive back door. They entered a wide hallway paneled with highly polished, dark wood. Staircases spiraled on both sides of the hallway to the upper floors. The doorman led Cassie to another door and downstairs to the basement. They passed through a large workroom, filled with washtubs and smelling of strong laundry soap and into a long, narrow room, filled with shelves of linens.

An imposing, dark-skinned woman emerged from behind a shelf. Cassie couldn't guess the woman's age, but her young-looking face was a marked contrast to the ample white hair visible around the edges of her mobcap.

"I'll take care of her now," the woman said, dismissing the doorman who turned and left.

She scowled at Cassie. "Well, what's your name?"

Cassie stood a little straighter. "Cassie Nichols is what I've always been called."

"I'm Zinnia, the housekeeper. I'm in charge of clothing and just about everything else in the running of this house. We all wear dark green here with a white mobcap, kerchief, and shift." She studied Cassie for a moment and went to the shelves where she looked through stacks of clothing.

Zinnia brought Cassie a petticoat and jacket, two white shifts, two mobcaps, two kerchiefs, two pair of underdrawers, and two pairs of stockings. "You're to wear your mobcap at all times, and the kerchief about your neck. Not on your head like the field slaves. You can change in here and leave your bag and the extra clothes on this shelf." She pointed to an empty shelf. "You'll be sleeping on the floor of Miss Adrianna's bedroom."

Cassie's heart, already aching, plummeted like a stone dropped into a well. It was bad enough to be thrown among strangers without having to sleep on the floor of a strange girl's bedroom.

4
Blanton Hall

Cassie looked around. "I'm to change here? What if the doorman comes b-back?"

Zinnia turned and busied herself with the linens. "Don't be silly. Mens don't dare hang around my storeroom. Hurry up and change."

Cassie glanced around again before taking off her clothes and placing them neatly in the tow bag. Then she put on the new shift, petticoat, and jacket. The jacket laced up the front and the sleeves came just below her elbows. It fit surprisingly well, and the expensive broadcloth felt soft and more luxurious than anything Cassie had ever worn. She secured the kerchief and arranged her hair under the mobcap before going to stand beside Zinnia. "What m-must I do for M-M-Miss Adrianna?"

Zinnia didn't look up from where she was refolding a blanket. "Anything she asks you to do."

"Will I have other chores?"

"Doin' for Miss Adrianna will keep you busy most of the time. And I wouldn't be surprised if Mrs. Blanton had something else in mind for you. If she doesn't have work for you, I will."

Cassie tried to keep her rising alarm out of her voice. "Has M-Miss Adrianna had a girl to wait on her b-before?"

Zinnia gave Cassie a hard stare that seemed to go right through her. "Calico's been takin' care of her. Now that Miss

Adrianna's seven, Calico's been sent back to the fields. It's time Miss Adrianna learned to be a lady."

Cassie had seen in Williamsburg how girls in wealthy families went from the nursery to being miniature adults. Her new mistress probably wouldn't be happy about leaving the nursery.

Zinnia continued, shaking her head. "I hope Mrs. Blanton is pleased. If she's not, you'll be sent to the fields, and that Horn, he's a devil. He never hesitates to use the whip on difficult slaves."

"Is Mrs. Blanton hard to please?"

"You may be all right, if you do all she asks. I'd heard she wanted someone who looked white and you most certainly do."

"But, I'm not white. B-Both my parents were people of color."

"You look white." Zinnia's voice was full of venom. "And how things look is very important to the Blantons."

No one at the Nicholses had ever mentioned Cassie's color. Her light skin and hazel eyes distinguished her from many slaves. It had never been an issue in Williamsburg, and it was something she couldn't do anything about. But her skin was obviously of importance, not only to the Blantons, but she guessed from Zinnia's disgusted tone it was important to her too.

Zinnia led Cassie to a sitting room with bright green wallpaper, gold-framed paintings, and gold and green, brocade-covered furniture. She had never seen, let alone been inside, such an elegant room. A China vase full of forsythia, just beginning to bloom, sat on the marble mantle. A woman and a young girl bent before embroidery frames. Cassie hoped her new mistress would be more welcoming than Zinnia had been.

The girl leapt from her chair, almost upsetting the embroidery frame. She was thin with mousy blond ringlets, heavy-lidded eyes, and a bad-tempered expression. She wore a yellow silk gown, similar to her mother's, and looked older than her seven years. The bright color of the dress made her skin look the color of a plucked, but uncooked, chicken. Cassie suspected Adrianna favored her father because her mother had dark hair, brown eyes, and pink cheeks.

"Adrianna, please sit," her mother said firmly. The girl looked sullen and sat down.

"What is your name, girl?" Mrs. Blanton asked Cassie.

Cassie struggled to say her name. "C-Cassie."

Mrs. Blanton looked annoyed. "Speak up, girl."

"C-Cassie Nichols." She spoke louder this time, but she still had trouble saying her name.

Mrs. Blanton now seemed more impatient than annoyed. "Cassie, if you do as Adrianna bids and you want to learn, you'll have no trouble here. Adrianna, you may show the new girl to your room. She can begin by organizing your clothes. Since Calico left, everything there is in a hopeless jumble."

Adrianna stood again. This time, she didn't disturb the embroidery frame. "Come along, Cassie," Adrianna said, mimicking her mother's imperious tone of voice.

Cassie followed Adrianna into the hallway and up the spiral stairs. Adrianna stopped at the head of the stairs. "You're not to use these stairs again. There are servants' stairs in the back of the house." She spoke with authority, as if she was used to giving instructions.

Cassie could feel tears coming again. She swallowed hard and held them back.

They walked down the hall and into a spacious blue room with long windows facing the York River, gray-green in the pale sunshine. Cassie glanced around. The four-poster bed with its embroidered blue and purple bed hangings was made, but aside from that, the room badly needed attention. A petticoat was on the floor and a gown lay in a heap on a chair. Doll dishes and crusts of bread littered a small table. Cassie wondered how long it had been since someone had tidied the room.

She bent to pick up the petticoat. "Don't do that now," Adrianna said. "Sabrina tidied the room this morning. I want you to play with me."

"M-Miss Adrianna, your m-m-mother wanted me to see to your clothes."

"What's the matter with you? You sound like a paper stuck in the spokes of a wheel."

Cassie had never been asked why she stuttered before. No one ever said much about it at the Nicholses'. "I don't know. I can't help it. I usually only have d-difficulty with certain words. Especially words that b-begin with *b, l,* and *m.* Sometimes *d* words, too. It's worse when I'm upset."

"Where did you learn your letters? Slaves aren't allowed to go to school."

"M-My father taught me. He attended the B-Bray school for slaves in Williamsburg."

"I don't like hearing you talk like that. Stop it."

"I don't do it on purpose."

"Well, I don't like it," Adrianna pouted. "My mother said you must do whatever I tell you. Now I want you to play."

"What would you l-like me to play?" Cassie was uneasy. When she was younger, she had sometimes played with children on Francis Street in Williamsburg, but they had played outside games such as tag and leapfrog. Her playing had ended as soon as she was old enough to work.

"You can be my horse." Adrianna gave Cassie a menacing grin. She picked up a riding crop. "Down on the floor."

Cassie dropped uncertainly to her hands and knees, appalled at Adrianna's demeaning command.

Adrianna climbed on her back. She clucked her tongue and dug her heels into Cassie's legs. Cassie moved slowly forward. Adrianna flailed her with the crop. Cassie winced from the sharp sting and kept moving.

"Faster," Adrianna commanded, hitting her again and again.

Adrianna was heavier than she looked. Cassie picked up her pace, but she soon began to tire. This was an awful game and she sensed Adrianna was doing it only to torment her. Cassie had been at Blanton Hall less than an hour and she already hated her new mistress.

5
Mary's Announcement

Late that afternoon, while Adrianna was having dinner with her family in the dining room, Cassie found her way to the kitchen, a separate building located beside the house. She hadn't eaten since morning, and Adrianna had occupied Cassie's every moment since her arrival at Blanton Hall. As she entered the kitchen, the smell of the freshly baked apple pies on the shelf near the window overwhelmed her with memories of home.

A broad-shouldered woman with a flat nose looked up from the pan she was scrubbing. "I'm Sophie, the cook," she said. "I guess you want something to eat."

The cook's manner was so unwelcoming that Cassie just stood near the door, uncertain what to do.

"Sit over there, out of the way." Sophie pointed to a small table off to one side. "I'll fix you something." Sophie grumbled to herself as she heaped cold cabbage, cornbread, and a slice of ham onto a plate and put it before Cassie.

At breakfast, Cassie only picked at her food. Now she was so hungry, the cold meal tasted good to her. She was halfway through when the kitchen door opened.

A buxom, young white woman with a red face and large, capable-looking hands came into the kitchen. She looked at Cassie and smiled, showing crooked front teeth. "You must be Cassie," she said in a thickly accented voice. "I'm Mary. I'm going to teach you to dress hair."

Cassie dropped her fork onto her plate in astonishment. The clatter of the fork made Sophie turn and glare at her. Cassie had never imagined being trained as a hairdresser. She knew the wealthy shaved their heads and wore wigs. But it never occurred to her that someone was needed to tend the wigs.

Mary took a plate from a shelf and served herself dinner. Then she sat down on the chair next to Cassie and began to eat.

Cassie had never sat at a table before with a white person. She picked up her fork and turned to Mary. "D-Dress hair?"

Mary looked at her curiously for a moment. "I guess no one bothered to tell you. I'm Mrs. Blanton's hairdresser. My indenture is almost up, and I'm to train you to take my place."

A wave of nausea hit Cassie. As hungry as she was, she could eat nothing more. Of course, no one had bothered to tell her anything. She was only a slave, a slave who would have to spend her life doing whatever her owners told her to do, whether she liked it or not. She had seen indentured servants in Williamsburg, but she'd never talked to one. Some people said they were little better than slaves. Cassie didn't believe that because they were white, and after seven years their term of indenture was usually over. She struggled to respond to Mary. "B-But I d-don't know anything about d-dressing hair."

"You'll have to learn. In the fall, Adrianna's brothers will go to the College of William and Mary, and she'll get a governess. She won't need you then. And when I leave, you'll be the family hairdresser. You'll take care of the wigs, cut hair for the household staff, and dress Miss Adrianna's hair until she gets her first wig."

"When will you teach me?" Cassie asked, wondering how she could ever get away from Adrianna long enough to do anything.

"Her Majesty has lessons most afternoons with Mr. Turner, her brothers' tutor. You'll report to me then."

Cassie realized her future had been all planned out, even to the time she would have hairdressing lessons. "M-Miss Adrianna didn't have a l-lesson today."

"'Twas because of your arrival. But I'll warrant she'll be back at her studies tomorrow afternoon."

Mary cleaned her plate in a few swift mouthfuls, stood, and placed it on a stack of dirty dishes. "You best be getting back," she warned as she was leaving the kitchen. "The Blantons will have finished eating and Her Majesty will certainly have plans for you."

Cassie put her dishes with the others and headed for the big house. A large spider's web in one of the boxwoods near the door glistened in the last rays of the sun. A yellow and black butterfly was caught in it. That's me, she thought. A tear slipped out of her eye and rolled down her face.

Adrianna was sitting at an embroidery frame in her room. "Mother has said I must practice my needlework," she said. "Here, *you* do it. I don't like sewing." She tossed a piece of embroidery to Cassie. "And mind you make neat stitches, or I'll be in trouble."

Cassie had never done embroidery. Fortunately, Aunt Ida had taught her to sew, and she knew how to make neat stitches. She soon saw what was required.

While Cassie carefully made cross stitches, Adrianna pulled all her toys out of a chest at the foot of her bed. Cassie wasn't sure if Adrianna was looking for something or just taking things out to plague her.

By bedtime, Cassie had run out of the nervous energy that had carried her through the day. She longed to get away from Adrianna and have the chance to rest and think through everything that was happening. Instead, Cassie helped Adrianna undress and put away her clothes. "You have to brush my hair," Adrianna said.

Cassie picked up the ivory-handled brush and pulled it tentatively through Adrianna's snarled hair.

"Ouch, that hurts!" Adrianna pulled her head away. "Haven't you ever brushed anyone's hair before?"

"No, M-Mistress." Cassie wanted to say she didn't want to touch anyone's hair, especially Adrianna's. But she remained quiet, taking a strand of Adrianna's hair in her hand while she carefully worked on a snarl.

Cassie wasn't sure what dressing hair would involve, but the very thought of having to do it day after day, year after year, until she was as old as Aunt Ida made her stomach churn. She continued brushing Adrianna's hair, and it seemed a long time before she could run the brush through it with ease.

Adrianna climbed into her high bed and Cassie stood beside it, wondering what she was to do now. "There are blankets in the bottom of the highboy." Adrianna pointed across the room. "You're to make a pallet on the floor. You must be close in case I need you in the night."

Cassie found two blankets and spread one on the floor, wanting nothing more than to be anywhere else. Adrianna blew out the sole candle that lit the room. In the dark, Cassie undressed and got down on the floor, using the other blanket to cover herself. Cassie expected at any moment Adrianna would call for her and she would have to run an errand.

In a few minutes, Cassie heard Adrianna breathing softly. As tired as she was, Cassie found it difficult to sleep, and she turned this way and that on the hard floor, trying to get comfortable. Her heart ached. She missed Aunt Ida and Moses. And what if she couldn't learn hairdressing? Would she be sent to the fields?

6
Hairdressing

The next morning Cassie again struggled with Adrianna's unruly hair. Cassie's fingers felt as big as turnips as she tried to sweep Adrianna's hair into an updo and secure it with pins.

"Leave the hair," Adrianna finally said irritably.

Cassie helped Adrianna on with her mobcap, tucking her hair beneath it. Still strands of hair hung limply on the nape of Adrianna's neck. Adrianna had difficult, uncooperative hair. Again, fear gripped Cassie. How would she ever learn the skills that would keep her from being sent to the fields?

Adrianna glared at her. "Don't stand there daydreaming. Help me dress. Where's my clean shift? You should lay out a clean shift and stockings every morning for me. They're kept in the Chippendale highboy."

Cassie went to get Adrianna's clothes, thinking she sometimes sounded just like her mother. Cassie took out a clean shift and stockings and handed them to Adrianna.

Adrianna slipped into her shift and pulled on her stockings. "Next, my stays."

Cassie picked up the whalebone stays where Adrianna had dropped them the night before. "You are to put away my clothes each night," she snapped.

Cassie wanted to ask when she was supposed to take care of Adrianna's clothes if every second her mistress had her doing something else. She bit her tongue to keep from saying anything.

She helped Adrianna on with the stays. "Tighter," Adrianna said as Cassie drew in the laces that secured the whalebone stays. "More or I'll grow up with a wide waist." Cassie pulled the stays tighter still, glad she didn't have to wear them.

Adrianna chose a blue gown and fancy shoes with silver buckles. Cassie helped her with the gown and knelt to tie her shoes.

Adrianna looked in the mirror. "I guess this will have to do until you learn to comb my hair." She headed for the door. "While I'm at breakfast, you're to empty the chamber pot, make the bed, and take my dirty clothes to the laundry." Adrianna left without bothering to shut the bedroom door.

Cassie allowed herself a deep sigh. Her stomach growled and she wondered when she would eat. After folding the blankets that made up her pallet, she began making Adrianna's bed. She had never realized how good her life in Williamsburg had been. The thought of mornings with Aunt Ida and Moses brought tears to her eyes.

In the afternoon, Mary came for Cassie, and she followed the hairdresser to a small room.

"This is the Missus' powder room," Mary said. "You're not to powder wigs anywhere but here."

The powder room had lilac-sprigged wallpaper, a dressing table, a chair, and a table.

"We'll practice on these." Mary pointed to two wigs on blocks. "The Missus likes the high roll, and she has these hairpieces for greater height."

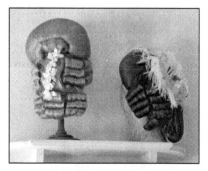

Women's wigs, Colonial Williamsburg
Author Photograph

Mary handed Cassie a heavy hairpiece. Cassie was glad she didn't have to wear one of them or the pinching stays.

Mary continued, "The Missus wants her hair to be higher than anyone's in the room. She'd like Miss Adrianna's hair to look fashionable too, especially when there are guests or they go calling."

Cassie had seen women with elaborate hairdos going into the Governor's Palace in Williamsburg. She had never imagined having to create such a hairdo herself. Hairdressing looked difficult, and Cassie again wondered if she would be able to learn to do it.

"Hairdressing is an art," Mary said as if reading Cassie's mind. Mary picked up a comb, took a hairpiece from a shelf, and began combing it. "Not everyone is good at it. I don't know if you'll have the right touch or not."

Cassie watched her a moment before asking, "What if I'm not good at it?"

"I can't say what Mrs. Blanton will do. I'll teach you the basics. The rest will be up to you."

Cassie noted a hairpiece the color of Adrianna's hair. "Does M-M-Miss Adrianna wear a hairpiece?"

Decorative hairpieces, Colonial Williamsburg

Author Photograph

"On special occasions. On most days, you just have to comb her hair. She doesn't have very nice hair. However, you'll have to learn to curl it and make it presentable."

"Curl it?"

Mary picked up an iron tool that looked something like scissors without blades. "This is a curling iron. You heat it in the fireplace. Not too much, mind you. Then you crimp her hair like this."

Mary took a strand of the hairpiece and illustrated the technique. "Of course, since it's not hot now, it won't make a curl. You have to be awfully careful not to burn Adrianna's hair. When you wash her hair, you can put in these curlers." She picked up a white curler about two inches long.

"How do I get them to stay in?"

"With rags. You just tie them."

The prospect of hairdressing seemed overwhelming to Cassie. She couldn't imagine having to do Mrs. Blanton's wig. "Where do I b-begin?"

Mary pulled off her mobcap, took pins from her hair, and with a few movements swept it into a fashionable hairdo. "Now you try." She handed the comb to Cassie.

She ran the comb through Mary's thick, blond hair and tried to put it up, struggling to secure it with hairpins. Mary's hair seemed to have a mind of its own. It refused to stay where Cassie put it. The pins she put in fell out and Mary's hair fell onto her shoulders.

Tears welled in Cassie's eyes and she shook her head. "I can't do it."

"Oh yes you can. It just takes practice that's all. Try again."

Cassie combed Mary's hair. She still couldn't seem to make the hair obey her wishes.

Mary threw up her hands. "Enough for now," she said, taking the comb and in two swift movements swept her hair up and pinned it.

Cassie returned to Adrianna's room with a heavy heart. She had not yet been with the Blantons for twenty-four hours, and it seemed she had been away from Williamsburg for a year. She longed to run to Aunt Ida, as she had when she was little, and feel Aunt Ida's comforting arms around her. She began putting away the toys Adrianna had dragged out that morning, her tears almost blinding her as she worked.

7
The Ball

In the days that followed, Cassie had daily lessons in hairdressing, and Adrianna's demands filled up the rest of her time. She made progress with her lessons, although Mary made it obvious to her that she had no special talent for hairdressing.

The weather grew warmer, and everyone at Blanton Hall became preoccupied with the coming spring ball. The slaves spent days cleaning and cooking in preparation for an elaborate midnight dinner.

Guests began arriving on Wednesday for the Saturday ball. There wasn't a guest room at Blanton Hall, but the family opened their bedrooms, and by Wednesday evening every bed, including Adrianna's, held three or four visitors. Trundle beds, taken out of storage, filled the empty spaces in the bedrooms.

The day of the ball, Blanton Hall buzzed with excitement. Cassie spent most of the day helping Sophie in the kitchen. She peeled and cut potatoes, washed and diced carrots, and it seemed good to be doing chores like those that she'd often done with Aunt Ida. After dinner she left the kitchen to get Adrianna ready for the ball.

She saw Mary in the hall on the way to Adrianna's room. "I'm worried about getting Adrianna's hair right," Cassie confided. "I've practiced on her as m-much as I could, but she doesn't like me fussing with her hair."

"You'll do fine. Just remember the things I've taught you," Mary said, hurrying in the direction of Mrs. Blanton's dressing room.

"Where have you been?" Adrianna demanded as soon as Cassie entered the room. "I'm ready for you to do my hair."

She didn't answer. Adrianna was obviously out of sorts since Cassie hadn't been at her beck and call all day.

Taking the curling iron, the combs, pins, and ribbons from a basket, Cassie put the curling iron into the fire.

"While it warms, I'll lay out your clothes for the b-ball."

She placed Adrianna's new rose-colored dress on her bed. Then she helped Adrianna on with her stays, stockings, and silk shoes. Realizing that the curling iron was ready now, Cassie took it from the fire and tested it by spitting on her finger and lightly touching it.

"Please sit," she said.

Adrianna sat in the chair in front of the mirror. A loud rumble came from outside and Adrianna jumped up and ran to the window. "A storm's coming," she said, returning to the chair.

Cassie waited for Adrianna to settle down, and then began curling her limp hair.

A louder clap of thunder shook the house. Adrianna lurched, the hot iron touching her neck.

She leapt up, screaming as if all the devils in hell were after her. "You burned me! You burned me on purpose!" She hopped from one foot to the other and screamed again. "You burned me!"

Cassie backed away from her enraged mistress. She heard a commotion in the hall. Zinnia, Mary, and Mrs. Blanton rushed into the room to where Adrianna stood with her hand over the burned spot.

"What's going on?" Mrs. Blanton demanded, her lips set in a hard line.

"Look at this!" screamed Adrianna, pointing to a red spot about an inch long by half-an-inch wide on her neck. "She did it on purpose. She hates me!"

Horrified, Cassie began to tremble. She placed the offend-ing iron back in the fire. She wanted to protest that it was an accident, she hadn't meant to hurt Adrianna, but the words strangled in her throat and she could say nothing.

Mrs. Blanton rushed to examine the burned place on Adrianna's neck. Her eyes bulged and she glared at Cassie. "Zin-nia, get that careless girl out of here!"

Zinnia strode over to where Cassie stood, cowering. Zinnia grabbed her by the ear and dragged her from the room.

"B-But . . ." Cassie finally was able to spit out as Zinnia led her down the stairs.

"Hush yourself. You've ruined the ball for Miss Adrianna and maybe her mother, too."

Cassie's ear throbbed and burned as Zinnia propelled her out of the house, across the yard and to the smokehouse. Zinnia opened the door, and shoved her inside with a deep sigh. "You'll be punished for your carelessness." She slammed the door and Cassie heard the scrape of a key in a lock.

Putting her hand to the ear, Cassie tried to ease the pain pounding through her head. Everything had happened so quickly, it seemed impossible to take it in. The smokehouse was dark and smelled of wood smoke. Lightning flashed, and Cassie momen-tarily saw a half-dozen hams hanging from the ceiling. A loud roar of thunder followed. She felt for the rough wall and slowly lowered herself to the floor. She was in a fix now. If Adrianna missed the ball, she would never forgive her. Maybe the curling iron had only grazed Adrianna's skin. With a sinking feeling, Cassie guessed that was only wishful thinking. Adrianna was burned, and it was all her fault.

The darkness grew deeper. Cassie heard scratching nearby. She knew rats sometimes got into smokehouses. Her heart ham-mered in her chest. She wanted to run, but she was trapped, a prisoner in the smokehouse.

Rain came, hitting the roof like bullets. The storm passed quickly and in the quiet after it, Cassie heard distant music. She grew more and more worried. Would she be sent to the fields or sold south? Zinnia had warned her that Horn whipped difficult slaves. She had seen him walking to the fields carrying a cat-o'-nine tails, and the very sight of the ugly whip had frightened her. She imagined the whip cutting her skin, drawing blood.

Hours passed. Cassie dozed and dreamed she was being whipped. She awoke when she cried out in her dream. Her heart was palpitating and even though the smokehouse was chilly, a trickle of cold sweat ran down her back. She closed her eyes, trying to calm herself with thoughts of Aunt Ida. How Cassie longed to see her, tell her everything. After a long while, she slept again.

A thin light came through the louvered door of the smokehouse. Cassie rubbed her eyes and the stiff neck she had developed from sleeping sitting up. Her mouth was dry and her stomach empty. As she came fully awake, the fears of the night before returned. What would happen to her? How long would she be kept here?

It seemed like a long time before Cassie heard the key turn in the lock. The door opened and a flood of sunlight momentarily blinded her.

"It's Zinnia," a voice said. "The ball's over. Everybody's going home today."

"How's M-M-Miss Adrianna?"

"Just a little burn. It sure enough hurt. But it's not serious. She carried on so her mother wouldn't let her go to the ball. Her red eyes and nose looked worse than the burn. She's fit to be tied. Of course, she says it's all your fault."

Cassie looked questioningly at Zinnia. "What'll happen to m-me now?"

"That's up to Mr. Horn. First, you need to change into your old clothes." Cassie noticed for the first time that Zinnia was carrying her tow bag.

Cassie swallowed hard. She was probably going to be whipped and then sent to the fields. Her legs almost gave out as she followed Zinnia along a rutted road to the slave quarters, a cluster of rough-hewn, one-room cabins in a ravine behind the stables.

They neared one of the slave cabins. "You'll change in my cabin," Zinnia said. "Come along inside."

Cassie was surprised to see that the high and mighty Zinnia had a cabin no bigger or nicer than the other slaves. It had only one room with a fireplace along the far wall, a dirt floor, and a loft. There was no glass in the two windows facing the rutted road. A bed covered with a patchwork quilt filled one side of the room while a rough table, a bench, and chair made up the rest of the furniture.

"Horn doesn't like to be kept waiting. Hurry out of those clothes," Zinnia said.

Cassie took the coarse shift and faded petticoat she had worn every day in Williamsburg out of her tow bag and felt for the reassurance of the coins Moses had given her. She groped in the bag. Her heart seemed to flip upside down. The coins, a reminder of her other life, were gone! Had Zinnia taken them? Or was it someone else? Whoever had taken the coins had pawed through her bag, the only thing that belonged to her. That seemed to Cassie to be the final blow, as old folks said, the last nail in the coffin.

Tears rose in her eyes as Cassie struggled into her old clothes. She folded the Blantons' clothes and put them in her bag. She had not washed her face or combed her hair since yesterday, but she told herself it didn't matter. Nothing mattered. There was no hope for her.

Cassie heard footsteps outside followed by a loud rap on the door. The overseer's pock-marked face was wooden and a sneer played around the corner of his month. He was carrying the cat-o'-nine tails. "Come with me," he ordered.

The world spun and Cassie grabbed at the doorframe for support. Steadying herself, she followed the overseer outside.

Early morning sounds came from the slave cabins they passed as the slaves got ready for a day in the fields. The overseer led

Cassie to a live oak tree in the center of the slave quarters. As they approached the tree, the slave quarters quieted.

"Face the tree," Horn barked, grabbing her hands and tying them tightly around the tree with a coarse rope.

The rough bark scraped the skin on Cassie's arms. She squinted into the morning sun, the sun and her tears all but blinding her. She waited for the first blow to fall. She heard voices behind her. Perhaps other slaves had been summoned to watch her punishment.

With a whoosh, the whip slashed her back, tearing her shift. Cassie winced from the burning pain and her feet wobbled as if they were going out from beneath her. She braced herself, trying to prepare for the next blow.

8
She Belongs to Me

Before the next blow fell, Cassie heard Adrianna's high-pitched voice. "No!" she yelled.

The next thing Cassie knew, Adrianna's thin arms were around her, shielding her from the next blow. "You mustn't hit her! She belongs to me. I don't want her scarred."

An awkward silence followed. Cassie heard the overseer muttering. "We'll see what your father has to say about this, Young Miss." Cassie heard heavy steps as someone wearing boots approached.

"My daughter's been plaguing me about what would happen to the girl." Cassie recognized Mr. Blanton's deep voice. "When I told her, she bolted from the breakfast table. Her sentiments are admirable, befitting the fine lady she will someday be." He paused and cleared his throat. "Cut the girl down and see that she's returned to Adrianna."

Cassie almost crumpled with relief. Horn's knife cut through the rope that tied her hands. She leaned against the tree for a moment to steady herself. She rubbed her hands where the rope had burned them and turned to see Adrianna walking toward the big house with her father.

The slaves who had gathered to watch the whipping began to leave, talking quietly among themselves. Zinnia led Cassie back to her cabin. Cassie carefully removed her clothes so as not to further inflame her burning back. Fortunately, as much as the lash had stung, she was grateful it hadn't drawn blood. She put on the green Blanton petticoat and jacket, stowing her old clothes in her tow bag.

As she dressed, Adrianna's words "she belongs to me" kept echoing in Cassie's mind. They were just a statement of fact, but the harsh reality of them stung her as much as the whip had. Her stomach churned. How could one person own another? She clenched her fists and vowed someday she would belong only to herself.

Twenty minutes later, Cassie, still weak in the knees, climbed the stairs to Adrianna's room, wondering what would happen now. The door was open. Her mistress sat by her bedside, holding her rag doll, Agnes, with a new doll in her lap.

Two eighteenth-century dolls, Colonial Williamsburg

Author Photograph

Adrianna stood up, holding on to Agnes and letting the new doll drop to the floor. Cassie rushed over and picked up the doll. The elegant doll looked like Adrianna. It was made of wood with glass eyes, human hair, a silk gown, and a fine cotton chemise.

"I don't like her," Adrianna said. "Mother gave her to me last night when I cried about missing the ball."

Cassie studied her mistress, trying to gauge her mood. It was unsettling to go from the whipping post to talking about dolls. Yet talking about dolls was better than revisiting the incident of the night before. "Why d-don't you like her? She's b-beautiful."

"Mother says I have to get rid of Agnes. Calico, my nurse, made her for me. Mother says Agnes is for babies and slaves, not for young ladies. Agnes is old, but she's soft. Not hard like this new one."

Adrianna's subdued manner and attention to the dolls was seemingly her way of avoiding the ugliness she had caused.

"It's not the new d-doll's fault," Cassie said.

"I told Mother that I'd give Agnes to you. But you really can't have her. You're just to pretend she's yours. This new doll is a grownup, and she hasn't been acting very grown up."

"What's she b-been doing?" Cassie asked.

Adrianna must have noticed her stuttering, but for a change, she didn't speak sharply about it. Instead she spoke to the new doll. "You've made a mess of sewing. Sit still and behave."

Cassie wanted to say that the new doll was very much like Adrianna, but she didn't dare. "What's her name?"

"I haven't named her."

"She has to have a name, even a name you really hate."

Adrianna frowned, as if thinking seriously. "Bertha, I'll call her Bertha."

"You should introduce B-Bertha to Agnes. Perhaps Agnes is l-lonely and would like a friend."

Adrianna held up Agnes who looked somewhat worse for wear. "I'd like you to meet Bertha. But you needn't worry. No one could ever replace you even though Mother says I mustn't sleep with you anymore."

Cassie, more than willing to play along, spoke for Bertha in a high-pitched voice. "I know I could never take your place. But perhaps we could be friends. Perhaps we can have adventures together." Cassie was surprised that when she pretended to be Bertha she didn't stutter.

As the pretending continued, Cassie's resentment of Adrianna grew. Sometimes she acted grown up, just like her mother; other times, like now, she acted like a spoiled young child. And Cassie had to guess at her mood and go along with it. Adrianna's overre-action yesterday had almost resulted in a whipping and Cassie's being sent to the fields. She knew she couldn't protect herself from Adrianna's fickleness. She would have to do something, but she didn't know what.

9
Pretending

During the next weeks, Cassie and Adrianna settled into a new routine. Cassie thought up adventures for the two dolls. Keeping Adrianna occupied made her life much more bearable. Her mistress wasn't as mean when she was busy. One July day, Cassie suggested the dolls have a fancy tea party.

"I'll dress Bertha while you go to the kitchen for tea and teacakes," Adrianna said with enthusiasm.

Cassie headed down the stairs and outside. The day was warm with a soft breeze blowing from the west. On the way to the kitchen, she glimpsed four British soldiers, dressed in their red coats and white breeches, talking to Mr. Blanton in front of the big barn.

She almost stopped and stared at them. In the months since she left Williamsburg, she'd heard little about the war. Blanton Hall had seemed an island, almost totally isolated from the rest of the world. Cassie had been so focused on just surviving she hadn't realized the British army was nearby. Was her father with them? Could she could get to the British and find him?

As she neared the open kitchen window, she overheard Zinnia talking with Sophie in a low voice. Cassie paused and listened.

"British soldiers have been raiding hereabouts. They've stolen cattle and freed slaves. But they haven't taken anything from here. I suspect Mr. Blanton's been hobnobbing with the British officers in town."

"Horn's afraid we'll run off. I overheard him asking Master what he should do," Sophie said.

The door opened and Zinnia bustled out of the kitchen. Seeing Cassie, Zinnia glared at her as she hurried off.

Zinnia's reaction made Cassie wonder if slaves were planning an escape. If so, she wanted to go with them.

Perplexed, but interested, she went into the kitchen. "Adrianna would like tea and teacakes."

Sophie grumbled to herself, but began to get the tea things ready.

As she waited, Cassie began working out in her mind how she might escape from Adrianna and Blanton Hall if the opportunity arose. She needed to learn more. She decided to linger in the hallways whenever she overheard people talking. Maybe she'd hear something else about the British or plans for escape.

Days passed and Cassie heard nothing more. Yet a certain tension hung in the air like summer humidity. You couldn't see it, but you could feel it, and it made her uneasy.

On Sunday, Adrianna went to church with her mother and father and then to dinner at a neighboring plantation. Cassie had a few hours of respite from her mistress's demanding company and decided to seek out Zinnia. She was the only slave Cassie knew well enough to ask about the British and the possibilities of escape. If any slaves were making plans they hadn't shared them with her. Perhaps if she lived in the slave quarters, instead of Blanton Hall, the other slaves would trust her. She didn't like the unfriendly housekeeper, but Cassie guessed if there was a plan for escape, Zinnia would know about it.

Zinnia wasn't at her cabin and Cassie walked through the quarters, finding them strangely quiet. Three small children played in a mud puddle and an old woman, smoking a pipe, sat in a rocker on a rickety porch watching them. "Where's Zinnia?" Cassie asked.

The old woman took the pipe from her mouth, and pointed. "They're all behind the big barn."

As she approached the wooded area behind the barn, Cassie heard hushed voices. A handful of slaves, grouped around Zinnia, stood in the cool shadows. Cassie joined them, standing beside Sophie.

"We won't make it," a gray-haired man said.

"We won't make it if we don't try," Zinnia said. "And if all of us go that can go, even if they catch us, what can they do to us?"

"Plenty," a heavy-set woman said, "we'll get a whipping." She fanned herself with a leafy branch and looked at everyone with pursed lips.

"If they beat us all half to death, they'll have no one to do the work," Zinnia replied, her eyes blazing. "The more of us who strike out for the British, the better chance we have of finding them and of not getting severely punished if we're caught."

A muscular young man, dressed in tattered trousers, confronted Zinnia. "What's your plan?" he asked.

"The plan will only be told to those who are coming with me. You need to make up your minds."

The slaves dispersed, talking among themselves. No one spoke to Cassie. She slowly walked back toward Blanton Hall alone, her mind in turmoil. No one had told her about the meeting. Clearly, she wasn't invited to join the others in the escape they were planning. She kicked a branch that had fallen onto the path and watched it tumble into a ditch.

Nearing the big house, Cassie saw the Blantons' carriage coming up the drive. In minutes, Adrianna would be looking for her. Cassie hurried to Adrianna's room and began tidying it.

Adrianna arrived a few minutes later, took off her pretty bonnet, and dropped it on the floor. Cassie hurried to pick it up, her mind on the British, just miles from Blanton Hall.

"Today we heard a story about Moses in church," Adrianna said. "The king of Egypt had ordered the male children of all the Jews killed, and the baby Moses was saved from death when he was placed in a basket and set adrift on the Nile River. Pharaoh's daughter, bathing with her maids, rescued Moses from the bulrushes and raised him. He became a great leader of the Jewish people."

Cassie knew the story, having heard it a number of times from the Moses she had lived with in Williamsburg. She noticed Adrianna had omitted the part about Moses delivering the Jews from slavery.

"I want to be pharaoh's daughter, and Agnes can be Moses. We can use these," Adrianna said, inspired by the story. She took the linens she used for drying her face and hands.

This was the first time Adrianna had thought up a pretend game and Cassie had no choice but to go along with it. "M-Maybe we'd b-better use old cloths."

"We'll use these." Adrianna began fixing the linens around her doll.

Cassie played the pretend game with Adrianna, thinking not about the baby Moses, but Moses, the grown man, who had led the enslaved Israelites to freedom.

Later at bedtime, lying on her pallet, troubled thoughts descended on Cassie like a flock of hungry blackbirds on a berry bush. She longed to escape, but many uncertainties filled her mind. What if the others wouldn't take her with them? And what if she escaped and the British wouldn't take her in? If she was caught running away, she doubted Adrianna would be able to protect her for so grave an offense. She cringed, remembering the sharp bite of the whip on her back.

Cassie wished she could talk to Aunt Ida and Moses. How she missed them. She had never had to make an important decision before. Slaves and children had everything decided for them. She didn't want other people always telling her what to do. But it would be nice to talk with Aunt Ida and hear Moses' wise advice.

But there was no one to help her. If she was to become her own person, she must begin now. She must decide what to do and live with the consequences.

Cassie drifted into an uneasy sleep only to wake before dawn. As she thought everything over, she made a decision. She would find a way to go with the others, even if they didn't want her along. She couldn't pass up the chance, no matter how slim, of finding her father. She'd talk to Zinnia. As the birds began their morning chorus, Cassie planned what to say to the housekeeper.

Later that morning, Cassie was returning Adrianna's cleaned chamber pot to her bedroom when she met Zinnia in the hall. "I want to go with you," Cassie whispered.

Zinnia put her hand to her mouth. "You can't go," she hissed under her breath. "You trying to sneak out of the big house would put us all at risk."

"I'll tell," Cassie said, knowing she would never tell on the others, but Zinnia didn't know that.

Zinnia gave Cassie a look that would wilt just-picked lettuce. "Behind the barn after the moon sets." Cassie turned and hurried away, her heart beating wildly. This was her chance.

10
Flight

The day seemed impossibly long to Cassie. She had not realized the plans for escape were so immediate. She didn't waver in her decision, but as the day dragged on, anxious thoughts tormented her. Would Horn unleash dogs to find her? She had heard the bellows of dogs chasing runaways, and the Blantons kept a pack of hounds. She had seen slave patrols in Williamsburg, and the patrollers had been rough men from the lowest class of society, the outcasts of the town. What would they do to her if they caught her?

By evening, Cassie's agitation had grown so much she was stuttering more than usual. What if Adrianna noticed and guessed something was up? Cassie made up a pretend game, but she couldn't keep her mind on imagining that Bertha was ill and Agnes was nursing her. More than once, Adrianna grew impatient with her and sent her on errands. Each time Cassie went into the hall, she checked the hands on the tall grandfather clock.

Finally, it was time for bed. Cassie put away Adrianna's clothes and got out fresh ones for the morning. Once everything was in order, she brushed Adrianna's hair.

"That hurt!" Adrianna complained when Cassie pulled on a snarl, trying to free it. "You're not paying attention. All evening you've been here, but your thoughts are somewhere else."

Cassie knew she had to say something. "I've b-been thinking about my father."

Adrianna gave her a curious look. "You have a father?"

"Of course, everybody does."

Adrianna's disdainful look helped to quell the many doubts Cassie had about running away. She realized Adrianna didn't even think of her as being human.

"Who does he belong to?" Adrianna asked.

"I don't know," Cassie said truthfully. She wanted to shout that he was free, that he'd gotten his freedom from the British, but she held her tongue.

"You are supposed to think about me, not him. You belong to me." Adrianna turned to face her mirror. "Be more careful from now on."

Adrianna's hateful tone strengthened Cassie's resolve to escape. She finished brushing Adrianna's hair and got her mistress into bed. Then Cassie spread the blankets for her pallet on the floor, she hoped for the last time.

Cassie knew she shouldn't sleep. She didn't know what time the moon set, but she didn't want to miss it. She lay still for a long time until she heard Adrianna breathing quietly. Then Cassie silently got up and sat on the floor near the long window. She closed her eyes and listened to the sounds in the house as it quieted for the night. Somewhere a door shut and she heard the murmur of voices from downstairs. After a while, the only sound was the tick tock of the grandfather clock in the hallway.

Awakening with a start, Cassie saw the moon gleaming through the opened window. The moon, like the sun, rose and set at a different time each day. She wished she had paid more attention to its cycle so she'd have some idea when it was going to set.

Cassie shifted uneasily on the hard floor, wide awake now, watching, waiting for the moon to set. Finally, the moon disappeared below the line of trees.

Making her way out of Adrianna's room, Cassie went cautiously down the stairs, avoiding those steps that creaked. If someone stopped her, she'd tell them she was going to the necessary. But no one was around. At the bottom of the stairs, she paused, held her breath, and listened intently. Hearing nothing, she headed to the storeroom, took her tow bag from the shelf, and with it held tightly to her chest, slipped outside.

In the thin light of the disappearing moon, Cassie ran toward the barn, her heart hammering like a hungry woodpecker pecking on a hallow tree. She rounded the barn and entered the ravine behind it. No one was there. What had happened? Was she too early or too late?

Moment by moment, it grew darker. Yet no one came. In the blackness, fear gripped Cassie like a hand from the grave as she realized no one was coming. Zinnia had lied to her. If the others had run away, they had done so in the moonlight. She had been stupid to think that anyone could run away in complete darkness.

What now? Her thoughts raced. The memory of the sharp bite of Horn's whip flashed into her mind. Should she return to Adrianna's room or head for Yorktown? She had come this far; could she reach the British without the others?

Cassie took a deep breath. Be calm, she told herself, and try to think clearly. Maybe this would be the only chance she might ever have of finding her father. She knew the road that ran behind Blanton Hall went from Williamsburg to Yorktown, and there were woods alongside it. She could stay on the road until she heard someone coming and then seek the cover of the woods. It wasn't much of a plan, but formulating it gave her hope.

With uncertain steps, Cassie hurried toward the road, barely visible in the faint light of the stars. She longed to go to Williamsburg, to return to Aunt Ida and Moses. But that would be the first place Horn would look for her. Any future she might have lay with the British army. She turned toward Yorktown.

Cassie walked and walked. Each step carried her farther from Blanton Hall, and as she put distance between herself and it, her nagging fears began to lessen. The August night was warm and alive with sounds of cicadas and chirping insects. Lightning bugs glittered like tiny candle flames. She wondered how long it would take to get to Yorktown, and she hoped she could reach the British before sunrise. Horn would be looking for her as soon as Adrianna awoke and found her gone.

The sky was beginning to glow in the east when she heard the telltale clip, clop of horses' hooves on the road. Her heart raced. Perhaps Horn was already after her. She ducked into the woods. The sounds grew closer, and Cassie thought she heard the rumble of wagon wheels. She peeked around a tree. A heavily laden wagon labored toward Yorktown. The wagon driver, his face half-hidden under a cocked hat, seemed focused only on the road ahead.

The wagon passed and disappeared. Cassie breathed a sigh of relief and returned to the road.

The daylight strengthened. Cassie noted with alarm that the farms along the way seemed to be growing closer and closer together. Certainly, someone would see her, stop her, and ask where she belonged. What should she do? Perhaps she should hide in the woods for the day, waiting until it was night to travel farther. She looked around frantically for a place to hide. Ahead was a patch of woods. She was just about to make her way into the woods when she rounded a bend and saw a cluster of houses ahead. She quickened her pace.

It was fully light now. Cassie looked down at her green jacket and petticoat. They were not the kind of clothes ordinary girls wore. She retreated into the woods, took off the Blantons' petticoat and jacket, and put on the old clothes she had worn in Williamsburg. She left the hated green jacket and petticoat in the woods.

As she neared the town, she saw the red uniforms of British soldiers ahead. A barricade stretched across the road. Stopped before it was the wagon Cassie had seen earlier. The soldiers were questioning the driver.

Cassie hesitated for a moment. She didn't know what she should tell the soldiers. Just then, behind her on the road, she heard horses, traveling fast. Then she heard someone yell, "That's one of them!"

A group of men rode toward her. She recognized Horn's slouch hat. For a moment, she panicked, not knowing what to do. She had no choice but to take her chances with the British.

Cassie ran, faster than she had ever run in her life, in the direction of the soldiers. She heard the horses behind her drawing closer. One of the soldiers at the barricade picked up his gun and aimed. Cassie almost faltered.

He was aiming the gun at her.

11
The British

Cassie kept running, her feet flying over the ground until she reached the barrier in the road. It took her a moment to realize the soldier was aiming not at her, but at the horsemen behind her. She was so out of breath she could hardly speak. She managed to gasp, "Help m-me, please."

Horn rode up to the soldiers. "This girl's ours," he said. "Her owners, the Blantons, are loyal to the Crown. She's no business with you."

An older soldier with a square jaw joined the soldier who still stood with his gun raised, ready to shoot. "What's going on here?" he asked Horn. "Explain yourself, sir."

"The girl's an escaped slave," Horn snarled.

"Our policy is to offer sanctuary to escaped slaves."

Horn's upper lip curled. "I'm sure if you bring this matter to your superiors, she'll be sent back where she belongs. Why not save yourself the trouble and turn her over?"

Cassie looked into the face of the British soldier talking with Horn. His brow was furrowed and he scowled at Horn.

"I repeat, our orders are to give sanctuary to escaped slaves." The soldier stood steadfast and eyed Horn with contempt. "You can lower your gun, private. This fellow isn't worth shooting."

Horn's face grew as red as a ripe tomato. "You popinjay! You cast-off scum of bedlam! You lobsterback! You've not heard the last of me!" Horn turned and galloped off, followed by the other slave hunters.

The soldier turned to Cassie. "Follow me, girl. We don't like Continentals, but we like slavers even less. That fellow's a nasty one."

Cassie, weak and shaken from her near capture, followed the soldier, not turning back to see what, if anything, Horn might do. His threats seemed to hang over her head like a flock of vultures. After all she had been through in the last minutes, perhaps, she wouldn't really be free after all. Perhaps the Blantons were such powerful Loyalists the British would return her to them. What might happen to her then was too awful to contemplate.

They entered the small town with its scattered brick houses and neat white church. Cassie was distracted from her dire thoughts by the sight of hundreds of red-coated soldiers. Was her father among them? If so, would she recognize him? As she looked from face to face, she became overwhelmed. She had no idea there were so many British soldiers in Yorktown. How would she ever find her father?

Her escort led Cassie to a barn where a group of exhausted-looking escaped slaves milled around listlessly or slumped on the ground. "You're to wait here with the others until somebody decides what to do with you," he said, turning and walking away.

Cassie looked around, feeling very much alone. Some of the runaways must have stolen their clothing since they were outlandishly dressed. A powerfully built man in an embroidered silk vest, wearing no shirt and slave trousers, lounged nearby talking to a dark-skinned woman. She wore a saucy yellow hat, decorated with a black feather, and a red silk dress. Then Cassie's gaze fell upon the familiar green of the household slaves at Blanton Hall.

Zinnia was standing near an empty horse stall. She spotted Cassie and came over to her. "I see you made it. Good for you."

"I almost didn't m-make it, thanks to you," Cassie said, emboldened by her escape and the fact Zinnia no longer had power over her. "Horn almost caught me."

Zinnia frowned. "I didn't trust you, especially after you threatened to tell on us."

"What happened to the others?"

"Blanton put guards around the quarters. Someone told him our plans. Was it you?" Zinnia glared at Cassie.

"No! I only said I'd tell so you'd take me along."

Zinnia sighed and shook her head. "Blanton neglected to put guards around the house or you and I wouldn't have made it. I was returning to the quarters when I saw the guards. I scurried back to the house, staying out of sight until it was time to run."

"What will happen to us now?"

"A lot of slaves from other plantations made their way here last night." Zinnia inclined her head in the direction of the others. "Someone will decide this morning who'll be able to stay."

"Do you m-mean they m-might send us b-back?"

"I've heard they only keep those fit to work. They mightn't keep a girl your size."

"Horn told the B-British that the B-Blantons would see that I was returned."

"I've never heard of the British returning any of the escaped slaves to their owners." Zinnia shook her head. "They won't return you to Blanton Hall, but they'll make you leave Yorktown, and that'll amount to the same thing."

Cassie looked around again at the other escaped slaves. A few small children played beside their mothers. Most were grown men and women, fit to work. She slumped to the ground suddenly wearier than she had ever been before.

It wasn't long before a pasty-looking soldier approached. "Come along," he ordered the assembled slaves.

Cassie stumbled to her feet and joined the other escaped slaves. The soldier led them to a table in front of a white tent where another soldier wearing a hat with a plume and a fancy uniform sat before a ledger.

Their escort made a mark in the sand with his boot. "Line up, here."

The slaves formed an uneven line. Cassie watched as each one gave a name and an occupation to the man who wrote their names in the ledger.

The sun climbed higher as the line inched forward. Cassie began to understand what was going on. The man was obviously some kind of officer. He directed those who said they were field hands to one side of his table where another soldier gave them picks and shovels. Others who had a skill went to stand at the other side of the table. A third group of older slaves, women with small children, and cripples stood forlornly under a nearby tree.

When Zinnia's turn came, she said she was a laundress and she went to the appropriate side of the table. Just before Cassie approached the officer's table, one of the men who had been at the barricade that morning came up to the officer and said something to him. The man indicated Cassie with a nod of his head and

British officer recording names in his ledger

Author Photograph with permission of Rex Hughes

she heard the words "important Loyalists." He was obviously telling the officer about the Blantons.

"Next," the officer said.

Cassie walked to the table, swallowing to moisten her dry mouth. She stood there a moment before the officer looked up. "Speak up, girl, if you're not dumb."

Words strangled in Cassie's throat. "I-I- I . . . ."

The officer held his quill poised over the ledger for a long moment. "Non-worker," he said. "Next."

Cassie's eyes filled with tears as she joined the slaves unfit for work. Beside her stood a man with one arm, and next to him an old woman, nearly bent double with age, leaned on a frail boy of about eight. The worst had happened. At the crucial moment, she had been unable to speak up for herself. Everything she had been through in the last hours had been in vain. She had reached the British, but they weren't going to let her stay.

12

A Skill

Cassie wiped tears from her eyes and looked around in desperation, hoping she could find a way to stay in Yorktown. It was then she saw Zinnia detach herself from the group of workers and approach the officer at the table. They spoke briefly, Zinnia gesturing in her direction. Zinnia returned to her place with the skilled workers, and the officer spoke to one of the soldiers nearby.

That soldier walked over to the non-workers. "You, the hairdresser's assistant," he looked directly at Cassie. "You're to join the others."

Cassie's heart leapt. She made her way to where Zinnia stood and looked up at her. The hard lines in the older woman's face had disappeared and she no longer looked angry. Cassie didn't know what to say. In spite of everything, Zinnia had spoken up for her.

Zinnia stood a bit taller. "I tol' the man you're a well-trained hairdresser and I tol' him what would happen to you if the Blantons got hold of you. He said he knew your owners were important Loyalists, but he doesn't hold with whipping children."

"Thank you. I'll b-be forever grateful to you."

Zinnia smiled at her. "I bet you never knew I was a laundress. That's where I got my start. And it is easier by far being responsible for clothes than it is for people."

Cassie thought back on her time at Blanton Hall. It hadn't occurred to her that Zinnia was so brusque because she too was unhappy. Zinnia, like every other slave, had a job to do, whether she liked it or not. Cassie realized also how important it was to have a skill, even if she wasn't particularly good at hairdressing.

The officer finished registering the escaped slaves, and a soldier took the former field hands away.

"They're going to be working on the fortifications being built around Yorktown," Zinnia explained.

A spindly black woman with a prominent Adam's apple approached the skilled workers. She wore a patched, homespun petticoat and a yellow kerchief. "I'm to see you all get to the right places," she said. "Come along."

"Where will we be staying?" Zinnia asked the woman as she led them away.

"We gots no tents or blankets. You're to make out the best you can. It's a good thing it's summer. The army'll feed you, and if you're lucky you may earn a coin now and again."

They came to a group of laundry women. Two women stirred steaming kettles of clothes they were boiling. Three others were scrubbing clothes in wash-tubs. Zinnia left to join them. She smiled and waved at Cassie. Zinnia seemed like a different person. She was a different person; she was free.

A woman doing laundry
in a British encampment

Author Photograph with
permission of Peggy Jennings

Under the shelter of a tarp, several women were kneading what looked like bread dough. Nearby another group was cutting and chopping vegetables. A huge shoulder of beef was sizzling on a spit, filling the area with smoke and the delicious smell of meat. Two of the recently escaped slaves joined the cooks.

"Where do you belong?" the woman in the yellow headscarf asked Cassie.

"I'm to help a hairdresser." The woman scratched her head, dislodging the bright headscarf. "That'll be Mrs. Byrdsong. Her tent isn't far from here."

They walked to a nearby tent. In front of it, a sturdy-looking woman with blue eyes and a ruddy face stood combing a wig. "Mrs. Byrdsong, I gots you a helper," the woman said, indicating Cassie.

"I hope she's better than the last one they sent me. I had no time for the likes of her," Mrs. Byrdsong said in a thick English accent.

Cassie left the group. Mrs. Byrdsong studied her for a moment and said, "You look a mite young to have had much experience with hair. What's your name?"

"I'm called Cassie."

Perhaps Mrs. Byrdsong looked a little like this re-enactor at Colonial Williamsburg.

Author Photograph with permission of Dolores K. Burke

Mrs. Byrdsong indicated the wig with her comb. "Well, Cassie, when I'm done here, you can show me what you can do."

Cassie stood watching Mrs. Byrdsong as she arranged neat rolls of hair on each side of the wig. Cassie knew how to do that. She hoped she could do it well enough to stay with the British.

Mrs. Byrdsong finished with the wig and put it back on a wig stand. She gave Cassie a good looking over again. "You're looking a little peaked. Are you all right?"

Cassie wasn't sure how to answer, but Aunt Ida had taught

her to be honest. "I've b-been up m-most of the night and I haven't eaten."

"I thought as much." Mrs. Byrdsong went to the campfire, stirred up the coals, and put a log on the fire. "There's oatmeal left from this morning. I'll warm it for you." She took a little water from a pail and added it to the pot with the oatmeal. "You sit right there." She indicated an overturned wooden box. "While the oatmeal's warming, we'll talk. You can tell me where you learned hairdressing."

Cassie sat and Mrs. Byrdsong pulled up a box beside her. Cassie told her as thoroughly as she could about Mary's training at Blanton Hall. "I'll b-be glad to show you."

"I'll take you up on that after you've rested," Mrs. Byrdsong said. "My hair's driving me half mad. I fix everyone else's, but there's no one to cut mine."

Cassie hoped her alarm didn't show. Should she tell Mrs. Byrdsong that she had only trimmed Mary's hair once? What if she made a mess of this woman's hair?

Mrs. Byrdsong went to the pot and stirred the oatmeal. "It's warm enough." She spooned the oatmeal into the bowl, and poured milk on it from a jug before giving the bowl to Cassie.

Cassie ate the steaming oatmeal, savoring its comforting taste.

"You were hungry," Mrs. Byrdsong commented as Cassie finished. "Would you like more?"

Mrs. Byrdsong took the bowl and refilled it before Cassie could say anything. She ate gratefully. She hadn't realized how hungry she was.

When Cassie finished, Mrs. Byrdsong indicated the pot with a nod of her head. "More?"

"No, thank you. That was very good." Cassie pointed to the women around the tents nearby. "I'm really surprised to see so m-many women with the army."

"There's a goodly number of us. If I didn't come along, I'd never see my husband, Sergeant Major Byrdsong. I might as well be a widow woman. Those of us who are legally married and work around the camp get half rations. My son's with the army too. I've two daughters, both grown, back in England. I can't wait 'til this war is over and we go home. I'm a grandmother three times over and I've never seen a one of my grandbabies."

"Your husband's a soldier . . . maybe he knows my father."

"Did your father come in with one of the early groups of escaped slaves?"

Cassie shook her head and told Mrs. Byrdsong about her father joining the British six years ago. "It m-may be silly, since he could be m-miles away now, but I keep hoping he's here."

"You poor dear, you have had it hard. I've heard that slaves who joined Lord Dunmore back in 1775 ended up in New York where they were released. So your daddy is probably nowhere around here. If he joined up again, he's probably with the army in New York."

Mrs. Byrdsong's information sent Cassie's heart into her shoes. There were so many soldiers here, why couldn't he be one of them?

"Now that you've finished, go inside the tent and stretch out. I changed the hay this morning. Have a nap. I'll call you later on. Then we'll see what you can do."

Cassie lay down in the fragrant hay and closed her eyes, never imagining her first day in freedom would be like this. As tired as she was, she tried to take it all in. Yorktown was a small town, smaller than Williamsburg, but it was full of soldiers and escaped slaves. From what Mrs. Byrdsong had said, in all probability, her father wasn't among them. Cassie didn't know where New York was, but she guessed it was a long way from here.

Outside the tent, Mrs. Byrdsong was speaking to someone about a wig. She seemed nice, but Cassie didn't trust white people. Mrs. Nichols had been nice to her too and Cassie had been traded to the Blantons. In this tent well within the British lines, Cassie was safe for now from Horn and the Blantons. But what would happen if she didn't cut Mrs. Byrdsong's hair correctly? Would she be sent out of Yorktown?

13
The Test

The sun was low in the sky when Cassie emerged from the tent. "Welcome back to the land of the living," Mrs. Byrdsong said heartily, taking off her mobcap and shaking out her hair. "I washed and dried my hair while you were sleeping." She handed Cassie a comb and a pair of scissors and sat on a box in front of her.

Cassie, still disoriented from having slept soundly, rubbed her eyes before beginning to comb out Mrs. Byrdsong's thick, auburn hair. The shadows were deepening and Cassie wished the light was better, but she was grateful to Mrs. Byrdsong for letting her sleep. "How m-much should I cut off?"

"Just trim it."

Cassie's hand shook as she held out the first strands of hair and snipped them off. She combed out the next section of hair and hesitated, trying to steady her nerves.

"What's the matter?" Mrs. Byrdsong asked.

"I'm afraid I'll m-make a m-mess of your hair. Then I'll be sent b-back to my owners."

Mrs. Byrdsong turned, faced her, and sighed deeply. "Nonsense. I'll not be the one to send a child into slavery. Now, get on with it. I've got a meal to prepare."

Cassie realized her fears of Mrs. Byrdsong had been unfounded. Her hand no longer shook as she continued cutting the older woman's hair. Snip. Snip. Snip. Comb. Check to see both sides were even. Snip. Snip. Snip.

"Do you have a m-mirror?"

"I don't." Mrs. Byrdsong felt her hair with her hands. "Feels fine to me." She stood and repositioned her mobcap.

Cassie smiled with relief. She had passed the test. The skill she had learned at the Blantons had saved her from being turned out of Yorktown. She returned the scissors and comb to Mrs. Byrdsong. "What do I do now?"

"It's time for you to join the other escaped slaves for the night. They're camped just over there in the field." She pointed. "But wait a minute before you go."

Mrs. Byrdsong went into her tent, rummaged around for a few minutes, and emerged carrying a piece of canvas. "Here, take this. I don't have an extra blanket, but I found this the other day in the encampment. I've been with the army long enough to know you never pass up something like this."

Cassie accepted the canvas. It was just big enough for her to sleep on or to use as a cover if it rained. "Thank you," she said.

"Run along now. I'll see you tomorrow after *reveille*."

Cassie didn't know what *reveille* was, but she guessed it was early in the morning. "Yes, ma'am. I'll be here early." She turned and headed in the direction Mrs. Byrdsong had indicated.

Cassie walked toward the field, relieved she had passed the test, but apprehensive at the same time. Everywhere she saw soldiers, guns, and the defensive lines, little more than mounds of earth. Common sense told her the British were preparing for a big battle with the Continentals. Would she be safe here if there was a battle? And what would happen to her if the Continentals won?

The field was filled with stubbles of last year's corn crop. It seemed liked hundreds of escaped slaves were standing about or sitting together in small groups. Cassie looked around for Zinnia, wanting to see a familiar face. She wandered about for several minutes before finding her, stretched out on the ground. Zinnia was awake, but stifled a yawn as Cassie approached.

"How'd it go?" Zinnia asked.

"All right. The hairdresser is nice."

Zinnia sat up and leaned on one elbow. "I gather we'll eat after the army's been fed. What is that?"

"A piece of canvas. Mrs. B-Byrdsong, the hairdresser, gave it to me."

"You better figure out a way to keep it with you all the time. I'd bet our brethren," she nodded in the direction of the others, "aren't to be trusted."

Cassie was tempted to say something to Zinnia about the theft of the coins Moses had given her. But Zinnia was the only person she knew here beside Mrs. Byrdsong. Someday Cassie would confront Zinnia about the coins. But today wasn't the day. Just hours ago, Zinnia had spoken up for her and Cassie had other things on her mind.

She pointed toward the nearest defensive line. "What will happen to us if there's a battle?"

Zinnia pursed her lips thoughtfully. "There's going to be a battle. No doubt about it. And I suspect one way or the other we'll be in the middle of it."

14
In the Encampment

In the days that followed, Cassie tried hard to please Mrs. Byrdsong. Cassie did what the older woman told her to do and found other ways to help out. She knew she was doing well because she overheard Mrs. Byrdsong bragging about her to the other women camp followers. And to Cassie's surprise, one day a woman whose hair she dressed gave her a penny tip. The tip reminded Cassie of her shillings. She had to find a way to keep her coin safe.

That afternoon when their work was finished, Cassie asked Mrs. Byrdsong, "Could I please b-borrow scissors and a needle and thread? I want to make a little pocket out of my old shift for my coin. I'm afraid I'll l-lose it or someone will steal it."

"A good idea," Mrs. Byrdsong said. "And I have a scrap of material that will be just the thing for it."

Mrs. Byrdsong went into her tent and when she came back, she had scissors, the needle and thread, and a square of red and pink patterned cotton. She held it out to Cassie.

"I couldn't take your nice m-material."

Two pockets for sale at the Margaret Hunter Millinery Shop, Colonial Williamsburg

Author Photograph

63

"Of course you can, it's just the thing. I want you to have it. And you can use a piece of your old shift to make ties to go around your waist."

"I've never made a pocket. But I know how they are made, and I've had a lot of experience sewing." Cassie thought back to the time when she had done Adrianna's needlework at Blanton Hall. Now she could sew something for herself.

That evening before it grew dark, Cassie began sewing the material into a pocket. Zinnia saw her sewing and came to where Cassie sat.

"I see you're making a pocket," Zinnia said.

Cassie's success working for Mrs. Byrdsong had made her secure enough to confront Zinnia. "Yes," she said, trying hard to keep anger out of her voice. "Someone at Blanton Hall took two shillings I hid in my tow bag. I don't want that to happen again."

Zinnia frowned and shook her head as she spoke. "You think I took your coins, don't you? Well, I didn't. I never stole your coins. I knew a slave in the household was stealing, but I never found out who it was. That's one of the awful things about being a slave. You never know who to trust."

Cassie realized from the pained look on Zinnia's face she hadn't rifled her tow bag.

"I'm sorry, Zinnia. Since you didn't trust *me*, I saw no reason to trust *you*."

Zinnia's face relaxed. "Then, I guess we're even."

It was not dark yet and since Cassie had needle and thread, she took out her mother's jacket. She had no secure place to keep it, so she'd alter it and wear it. She had often seen Aunt Ida altering clothes. Now she made two neat pleats in the back of the jacket so it would fit. When she finished, she modeled it for Zinnia.

Zinnia looked her over. "If I was going to take anything, I would have taken that jacket. It looks mighty fine on you."

The next morning was bright and sunny. Cassie put on her mother's jacket and after *reveille*, which she had learned was the early morning wake up call to the troops, went to find Mrs. Byrdsong.

"What a pretty jacket! You look like a young Colonist this morning," Mrs. Byrdsong said with a smile.

Cassie turned around for Mrs. Byrdsong to see the back. "The jacket belonged to my mother, and I thought it best I wear it. That way, no one will be tempted to take it." Cassie untied the pocket, took it from under her petticoat, and held it out for Mrs. Byrdsong to inspect.

Mrs. Byrdsong took the little pocket and looked it over. "Nicely done," she said.

Cassie, unused to praise, particularly from white people, stood a little taller and smiled with pleasure.

"We're taking an hour off. We're going to *assembly* today," Mrs. Byrdsong announced.

"What's *assembly*?"

"At *assembly*, the soldiers in the field troop the colors. The fifes and drums play. It's a kind of a parade. It's grand!"

Cassie wasn't surprised Mrs. Byrdsong was taking her to *assembly*. Once Cassie had proved what she could do and that she was a conscientious and careful worker, Mrs. Byrdsong had taken special interest in her wellbeing and education.

This morning as they headed to the parade field, Mrs. Byrdsong pointed out how much stouter the defenses were now. "See, they stretch all the way around the town."

The defensive line around Yorktown had grown day by day. Former slaves worked long hours creating higher and stronger dirt mounds. As the defenses grew stouter, Cassie worried more and more about the coming battle.

They arrived at the parade ground and Cassie searched the faces of the soldiers. She hadn't given up hope that her father was one of the thousands of British soldiers in the encampment.

British officer

Author Photograph with
permission of David Gobel

"They look and sound grand, don't they?" Mrs. Byrdsong said proudly. She indicated one of the drummers. "That's my Johnny."

The soldiers spent long hours each day caring for their equipment and uniforms. They did indeed look grand in their red coats and white breeches, with their guns glittering in the sun. Now Cassie looked where Mrs. Byrdsong pointed. Cassie had met Johnny briefly when he visited his mother, but today on the parade field she hadn't spotted him with the fifers and drummers. She had been too busy looking for her father in the ranks.

"And there's General Cornwallis!" Mrs. Byrdsong said, nodding in the direction of a group of officers.

General Cornwallis was the famous general who had crushed the Patriots at Camden. Now he was preparing the army to defeat the struggling Continental army again. Cassie studied the heavyset officer with dark eyebrows, a straight nose, and a pointed chin, who was the center of everyone's attention. She noticed right away he wasn't wearing a wig and his own hair was very white.

Standing with Mrs. Byrdsong, Cassie watched the well-turned-out troops pass, rank after rank, marching to the jaunty tunes of the fifers and drummers. The unfamiliar ceremony continued in a blur of flags displayed with clocklike precision. Cassie couldn't help but imagine her father taking part in *assembly*.

After the ceremony, they headed back to Mrs. Byrdsong's tent. "You're looking a mite sad," Mrs. Byrdsong said in her straightforward manner. "What's the matter?"

"I keep thinking about my father."

"This war will be over someday. All wars end, sooner or later. And after we win, you'll be able to find him. He'll probably have done well for himself, working for our side."

Cassie found it hard to share Mrs. Byrdsong's optimistic view. Day by day more Continental soldiers massed on the far side of the defenses. She hoped Mrs. Byrdsong was right and the British would win, but Cassie feared the worst. If the Continentals won, she and her father would be returned to slavery.

Back at Mrs. Byrdsong's tent, they began the day's work. Mrs. Byrdsong took a curling iron from the fireplace where it had been warming and handed it to Cassie. She pointed to a wig on a wig stand. "See what you can do with that awful-looking thing."

Cassie picked up a wig that looked like it had been slept in and then crushed into a ball. She began to try to recreate the curls. Mrs. Byrdsong was nearby cutting up onions and potatoes into a kettle.

It was a good opportunity for Cassie to ask Mrs. Byrdsong about the Blantons. She began tentatively. "While I was at B-Blanton

Preparing food in a British encampment

Author Photograph

Hall, raiding parties never visited there, and when I got here, the overseer from B-Blanton Hall said my former owners were I-loyal to the Crown. Do you think there's a chance they can reclaim me?"

Mrs. Byrdsong stopped putting onions into the cooking pot. "Whether or not those Blantons are Loyalists, they'll try to get you back by proclaiming their loyalty to the Crown. I don't think they stand much chance. They may be the worst kind of people, loyal to whatever side seems to be winning."

Cassie thought about this for a while. She hoped Mrs. Byrdsong was right. She never wanted to return to Blanton Hall. "There's something else on my m-mind."

Mrs. Byrdsong looked up from peeling a potato. "Spit it out."

"My father and I got our freedom by fleeing to the B-British and yet the Patriots are fighting for their freedom."

Mrs. Byrdsong chuckled. "I understand your confusion. There's no denying freedom is a good thing. And if we British hadn't allowed the colonies so much freedom, there probably wouldn't be a war now. I suspect once you get a taste of freedom, you don't like anybody telling you what to do."

"So, do you think the Patriots are right?"

"I didn't say that. They're disloyal and should be grateful for all we've given them. I'm just saying I think I can understand how they want to run their own affairs. Is there anything else on your mind?"

"The coming b-battle . . . ."

"Yes, that's worrisome. But I've told you Cornwallis is as good a general as there is anywhere."

"But what if we I-lose? I don't want to go b-back to b-being a slave."

Mrs. Byrdsong put a reassuring hand on Cassie's arm. "Now, now, we're sure to win. And if the world is turned upside down and we don't, I'm sure the army will honor their guarantees to the escaped slaves."

Cassie wanted to believe Mrs. Byrdsong, but her worries, like unwelcome guests, didn't go away. In her young life, she had learned the unexpected can sometimes happen.

A soldier Cassie had never seen before came to where they were working. Mrs. Byrdsong put down her paring knife.

"You've been reassigned," the officer told Mrs. Byrdsong. "You and your girl are needed to help with the sick."

Mrs. Byrdsong's face clouded. "That many are sick?"

"I'm afraid so," the soldier replied. "You're to report to the chief surgeon's tent at the hospital area tomorrow."

As soon as the soldier left, Mrs. Byrdsong turned to Cassie. "Things must be getting serious."

"What will I be doing?"

"Anything that needs to be done, the same as me."

This new and unexpected assignment confirmed Cassie's fears. Anything could happen in the days ahead.

15
The Field Hospital

Long rows of white tents made up the field hospital. All the tents were filled with feverish soldiers, many with chest-wracking coughs. Rumors that a battle was pending flew about like bats at sunset. Cassie wondered what the surgeons would do if they had to care for the wounded in addition to the numerous sick soldiers. Already, makeshift shelters made of canvas stretched over four poles were springing up around the hospital tents.

She found Mrs. Byrdsong shaving a deathly pale, young soldier, hardly old enough to have a beard. The older woman looked up as Cassie approached. "I'm almost done." Mrs. Byrdsong finished shaving the soldier, dipped the razor into the basin by her side, and then wiped it on a cloth.

"Do you need more water?" Cassie asked.

"I'm through here. But, I've volunteered to see to the slaves who have gotten the pox. Have you had it?"

Cassie shook her head. Just last night, Zinnia had told her more and more slaves were coming down with smallpox. She remembered when she lived in Williamsburg, people had gotten the pox and died.

"I thought as much. You're not to go near anyone with the pox."

A soldier rushed by them shouting. "Continental troops! They're surrounding the town!"

"There'll be a battle soon," Mrs. Byrdsong said. "Don't worry about it. I've been in more than one battle. And I've told you General Cornwallis is as good as they come. We're sure to win."

A group of women and former slaves, all talking at once, headed off in the direction of the defensive lines. Mrs. Byrdsong seemed unperturbed, but Cassie wasn't so calm. The memory of Horn's blood-stained whip flashed through her mind. If the Patriots won, she would be sent back to Blanton Hall and whipped.

Mrs. Byrdsong must have noticed Cassie's agitation because she said, "Run along and find out what's going on."

Cassie ran to catch up with the others. At the fortifications, she stood on her tiptoes to see. Thousands of Continental soldiers in blue uniforms were moving steadily forward. Soldiers in white uniforms moved forward on one side. At the same time, British troops in their red uniforms were withdrawing to an inner defensive line. It all appeared to be very orderly. She watched for several minutes before returning to report to Mrs. Byrdsong.

Summarizing what she had seen, Cassie concluded, "I'm not sure what's going on."

"Cornwallis has been waiting for the Continentals to come out into the open and fight. In most of our battles so far in the colonies, the armies met on a field and fought it out because the Continentals don't know much about siege warfare."

"Siege warfare?"

"The armies dig in and bombard each other until one side surrenders."

"Is that what is going on now?"

"That's what seems to be happening." A cloud seemed to pass over Mrs. Byrdsong's face. "The soldiers in white uniforms are French soldiers. And the French know how to conduct sieges."

Cassie wasn't sure she understood siege warfare, but she gathered from Mrs. Byrdsong's face that the arrival of the French made her more concerned than she had been in the past.

"I'm off to see what I can do for the slaves with smallpox," Mrs. Byrdsong said. "Please take these back to my tent." She handed Cassie the shaving razor, basin, soap, and several cloths.

Cassie walked toward Mrs. Byrdsong's tent, worrying about the coming battle. During her early days in the encampment, she had seen Sergeant Major Byrdsong often in the evening when he returned to Mrs. Byrdsong's tent after *tattoo*, the army signal that sent everyone to their tents for the night. But as she headed there now, Cassie realized she had not seen him for days. As she passed the long lines of soldiers' tents, she noticed they were hurrying about in a businesslike way. Before, they had often seemed relaxed and sometimes even jovial. She remembered one day when Mrs. Byrdsong's son, Johnny, the drummer, had visited his mother. Cassie had noted his drum with the taut leather across its head. Now as she looked around, it seemed to her that the whole town, surrounded as it was with barricades, was taut just like the drumhead.

16
Smallpox

The tension in the encampment didn't lessen. Even Mrs. Byrdsong, who usually was even-tempered, seemed out of sorts. As the days passed, Cassie's stuttering that had been improving steadily as she had become comfortable with Mrs. Byrdsong, grew worse. She tried to keep a positive attitude, but in the pit of her stomach, she sensed an impending crisis.

One evening as it grew dark, Cassie sought out Zinnia. They had become friendlier since their escape and generally spent the nights somewhere near each other. But for the last several nights, Cassie hadn't seen Zinnia. Now Cassie scoured the field looking for her.

It had been a bad day. General Cornwallis had ordered many of the horses killed since there wasn't enough forage in the besieged town to feed them. All day, Cassie heard the screams of the dying horses. The soldiers slaughtered the horses at the waterfront where the current would carry away their carcasses. It had been unsettling to everyone.

It was growing dark when Cassie spotted Zinnia seated by herself at the edge of the field, leaning against a tree stump.

"Don't come close," Zinnia called as Cassie approached. "I've got it."

"Got what?"

"The pox."

"How do you know?"

"I don't know for sure. But I've seen enough of it here in camp to suspect that's what's ailing me."

Cassie found it hard to believe someone as strong and apparently healthy as Zinnia could get the pox. "What can I do to help?"

"I'm going to make my way to the field hospital while I'm still strong enough to get there. I didn't want to leave without saying anything to you. But I didn't feel up to looking for you myself. I figured you'd find me."

Zinnia was obviously ill. "I'm so sorry, Zinnia," Cassie said truthfully. "Thank you for I-letting me know. I would have worried. I'll still worry, but at I-least I'll know where you are."

"I best go," Zinnia said, rising with difficulty.

"Mrs. B-Byrdsong has had smallpox, and she's been tending those down with it. I'll ask her to I-look for you tomorrow."

Zinnia managed a sad farewell smile and walked haltingly off toward the field hospital for escaped slaves.

It began to spit rain. Cassie crawled under her square of canvas, very much alone. She wondered if Zinnia had caught the pox from laundering linens for the sick soldiers and if being with Zinnia had exposed her to it. Cassie's stomach lurched. Perhaps she'd get the dreadful disease too. She was powerless; powerless to help Zinnia, and powerless to help herself.

It rained during the night, and the next morning, Cassie's clothes were wet when she returned to the field hospital. Her back ached from trying to keep dry curled up under the canvas. But there was so much for her to do, she soon forgot her own discomfort.

At midmorning, Cassie looked for Mrs. Byrdsong and found her hanging blankets on a clothesline. "These got wet last night," she said. "Sick folks out in the rain. It's awful."

Cassie went to help with the blankets. "Don't touch these," Mrs. Byrdsong warned. "They may be infected with pox."

Cassie backed up a bit. "Zinnia from B-Blanton Hall went last night to the field hospital to be treated for the pox. Would you m-mind looking for her and making sure she's being taken care of?"

"I can't." Mrs. Byrdsong's face was red and distorted. "I'm so angry I'd like to hit someone or something. I wish I had a stick to beat the blankets, but all the sticks, even the picket fences, have been used for firewood."

"What's the m-matter?"

"I can't see to your friend or any of the other slaves with smallpox."

Cassie's mind stumbled over the word *friend*. She had never thought of Zinnia as her friend. But aside from Mrs. Byrdsong, Zinnia was Cassie's only close acquaintance in the encampment.

Mrs. Birdsong continued. "We've no more room for them. Too many are sick. Cornwallis is turning them out."

"Turning them out? I don't understand."

"The escaped slaves who have smallpox will be sent out of Yorktown. That way they won't infect the soldiers and other slaves, and they just may infect the enemy."

Cassie couldn't believe what she was hearing. "I thought the B-British promised freedom to any slaves who would join them. If they're sent out of Yorktown, they'll either die or they'll be captured and returned to their owners. Maybe they'll even be killed by the Continentals!"

"That's why I'm angry. It's not right. Some of the escaped slaves have been with us since the Carolinas. They've worked in the scorching sun on the fortifications and helped in the encampment, doing the chores no one else wanted to do. And that's not all. I haven't seen it. But I've heard that the tide's brought back all the dead horses, bloated and stinking. You can't escape your evil deeds."

Zinnia's plight and that of the other sick slaves along with the horror of the bloated bodies of the horses turned Cassie's stomach. She struggled to come to grips with the situation. "What can I do for Zinnia?"

Mrs. Byrdsong's anger seemed to pass as she considered what needed to be done. "There's nothing you can do. She'll need food. I'll see about getting her some."

Later that day in stifling heat, Cassie stood near the outer line of defenses with other well slaves and watched in horror as the British soldiers prodded the sick slaves with bayonets, forcing them out of the encampment. Many were so weak they couldn't walk, and those less ill had to carry them. Some seemed half crazy with fever. Terrible pustules disfigured them all. Surely, the damned in hell couldn't suffer more than these smallpox victims.

She searched for Zinnia. Finally, Cassie saw her. Zinnia and another woman were walking together, leaning on each other for support. Zinnia, once so strong and healthy, looked so pitiful Cassie wanted to turn her eyes away, but she couldn't help but watch as Zinnia stumbled and fell, bringing the other woman down with her. Soldiers yelled at the two women and one nudged them with the butt of his musket, trying to force them to get up. Once they were standing again, another soldier thrust his bayonet menacingly near them.

Mrs. Byrdsong strode up to the two struggling women. Cassie couldn't hear what Mrs. Byrdsong was saying, but Cassie saw her gesturing for the soldiers to back off. When they did, she gave Zinnia a bundle. The tears that had risen in Cassie's eyes overflowed.

Mrs. Byrdsong, spotting her among the spectators, made her way to Cassie's side. "Come along. There's work to be done."

Cassie returned to her chores, sick at heart. She grieved for Zinnia and for all the slaves who took their chances with the British in order to obtain their freedom. The British had betrayed them. They had used them and now that the slaves were sick, the British were discarding them, like worn-out garments. She tried to think what she would do if she were cast out to fend for herself. Bleak thoughts filled her mind, and she didn't have any idea how she would manage.

17
The Bombardment Begins

Five days later on October 9, during the middle of the afternoon, Cassie was bathing the forehead of a feverish soldier with cool water when the American batteries opened fire. The roar of the cannon shook the earth. The soldier sat up, his eyes wild. Cassie, swallowing with difficulty, put the cloth into the basin and went to find Mrs. Byrdsong.

Cassie found her, carrying linens to the supply tent. "Don't be frightened, dearie. You'll get used to it," Mrs. Byrdsong said. "You don't get butter without a lot of churning."

Another burst of cannon fire exploded. Smoke and a foul smell filled the air. Cassie followed Mrs. Byrdsong to the supply tent and watched as she carefully stacked the clean linens. The shelling continued. Cassie wanted to cover her ears to shut out the terrible noise and to run to someplace safe, away from the belching, roaring guns.

Firing a cannon (from an eighteenth-century illustration)

Bowles & Carver, *Old English Cuts and Illustrations* (New York: Dover, 1970), p. 13

Mrs. Byrdsong had just finished when the cannons began to find their range. A cannonball hit a nearby tree, sending splinters everywhere. She grabbed

Cassie's hand, pulling her toward a small building that had once been a dairy.

"Sit on the floor, away from the window!" Mrs. Byrdsong gasped as they struggled inside the abandoned dairy.

They sat on the floor across from the building's one window. "This doesn't give us much protection, but it will have to do until things quiet down," Mrs. Byrdsong said, still gasping for breath. "When there's a lull, I'm sure they'll move the sick to somewhere safer."

The lull in the bombardment didn't come. Cassie winced every time a cannonball hit somewhere nearby and debris fell onto the dairy. Instead of letting up, the roar of the guns grew louder. "I think another battery has opened fire," Mrs. Byrdsong said after a while. "They're not going to stop. We had best try to make our way to the chief surgeon's tent for instructions."

Mrs. Byrdsong rose cautiously and opened the door. Cassie got up too. Holding on to the doorframe for support, she stood next to Mrs. Byrdsong and looked out. It seemed like the very sky, filled with fire and destruction, was falling. Mrs. Byrdsong grabbed Cassie's hand and they dashed out of the building. Tents and buildings were on fire and Cassie choked and coughed in the smoke-filled air. Soldiers and civilians ran in every direction.

Turning to see if Cassie was behind her, Mrs. Byrdsong yelled, "Stay close!" She looked around as if gauging where the next shots would fall. Cassie's knees almost buckled as she ran. They had only gone a little way when they almost stumbled over a wounded soldier, lying in a heap, moaning in pain.

Mrs. Byrdsong stopped and knelt. Cassie crouched down beside her, horrified at the sight of blood coming from what was left of the man's leg. Mrs. Byrdsong seemed to know what to do. She whipped off the clean kerchief she wore about her neck and expertly tied it tightly above the stump. The profuse bleeding stopped. She next tore a strip from her shift and bandaged the bloody stub.

Finishing, Mrs. Byrdsong stood. Cassie rose also, feeling dizzy and faint. "We'll find someone to help you," Mrs. Byrdsong told the soldier. "Try to lie still." The man nodded and gritted his teeth.

Mrs. Byrdsong charged off again with Cassie close behind her. They found the surgeons' tents. All was chaos. The surgeons worked feverishly in the fading light. Men lay about on stretchers, and more wounded seemed to be arriving every moment. Cassie heard blood-chilling screams and instinctively covered her ears. Two soldiers carried a man, kicking and screaming, with a gaping wound in his side into a tent where a surgeon was operating on one man after another. Tears sprang to Cassie's eyes and rolled down her face. War was horrible beyond all words. Whether or not the British could be trusted, no one deserved such terrible pain and disfigurement.

Intent on helping the wounded, Mrs. Byrdsong didn't seem to notice the death and destruction raining down on them. She told two stretcher bearers where the wounded man she had bandaged lay and then she swung into action.

"Cassie, find a pail and water," she ordered. "I'll be here doing what I can." Mrs. Byrdsong knelt beside a young soldier bleeding from the head.

Cassie hated to leave Mrs. Byrdsong's side. "Go, quick!" Mrs. Byrdsong yelled.

Her eyes burning and her throat choking from the smoke, Cassie made her way to where she remembered seeing a well. She found it and an abandoned pail. With hands shaking, trying to ignore the commotion going on around her, she attached the pail to the rope, lowered it into the well, and filled it with water. She began to pull up the pail. It took more strength than she knew she had, but somehow she managed. At the top of the well, she dropped the rope and grasped the pail with both hands. Water sloshed onto her petticoat. She bent over the pail and took a deep drink of the cool water before carrying it to Mrs. Byrdsong.

"Now find a cup," Mrs. Byrdsong said, briefly glancing up from a soldier she was bandaging, "and then start giving drinks to the wounded."

Darkness descended as Cassie began looking for a cup. Every soldier must have a cup, if only she could find one. She seemed in a daze as she looked around. A cannonball burst nearby and she fell to the ground.

18
Under Fire

Cassie got to her knees and then stood up unsteadily, shaking dirt from her petticoat. The cannonball had blasted a hole in the dirt only yards from her. People were running in every direction and frantic shouts filled the air. Cassie wanted to run to safety, but seeing no place offering shelter, she began searching again for a cup. She skirted the shell hole and stopped a woman carrying a small child. "Do you have a cup?" Cassie screamed above the thundering of the cannons.

The woman's eyes were wide with horror. She managed to shake her head no. Cassie next accosted a soldier. "I need a cup for the wounded."

"Look near campfires," the soldier shouted before hurrying away.

In the dim light, Cassie made out the faint glow of what hours ago had been a campfire. She searched around it without success. She checked several more and finally found a dented, but usable cup. She hurried back to where she had left Mrs. Byrdsong. She had procured a lantern somewhere and was bandaging a soldier's arm.

Without waiting for instructions, Cassie offered a drink to the nearest wounded soldier. "Water?"

The man raised his head. "Please."

Cassie gave the man a drink and moved on to another soldier, writhing in pain from a gaping wound in his neck. "Help me," the man gurgled.

Mrs. Byrdsong had just finished bandaging the soldier's arm. Cassie pulled her over to the soldier wounded in the throat and Mrs. Byrdsong bent to minister to him. Cassie took her pail and cup to another soldier who gratefully drank.

Hours passed, and the bombardment continued. The flickering of flames from fires burning all over Yorktown cast an eerie light over the hospital tents. Cassie refilled the water pail and continued giving water to the wounded. She became aware that they were being taken to the waterfront where the high banks along the York River provided a little protection from the bombardment. A terrible thought leapt to her mind. Perhaps the British would push the dead soldiers, like the horses, out into the river.

Time seemed suspended. The first rays of the sun appeared in the east and the cannonade didn't let up. Cassie filled and emptied one last pail of water and then fell in an exhausted heap beside a low stone wall. She couldn't go on.

The next thing Cassie knew Mrs. Byrdsong was gently shaking her. "I've been looking for you. It's not safe here. We're going to the waterfront."

Cassie looked up at Mrs. Byrdsong. Her mobcap was smudged with dirt or soot, and splotches of blood stained her gown. "What about the wounded?" Cassie yelled above the roar of the cannon.

"Most of them are at the waterfront now. Come on!"

Cassie hurriedly got up. Her arms and legs ached and she had no idea how long she had slept. Her stomach cramped with hunger and she realized it had been many hours since she had eaten. Trying to shake off her exhaustion, she grabbed her pail and cup and followed Mrs. Byrdsong who plunged down the steep bank to the water's edge. In the early morning light, the red leaves on the gum trees along the road to the river looked like splotches of blood.

The waterfront was crowded. "Even Cornwallis is here." Mrs. Byrdsong inclined her head in his direction. The general sat at a table near the mouth of a cave, studying a map.

"Be a good girl and fill your pail again. There's water in those casks." She pointed to a row of casks near the wharf.

Cassie didn't hesitate. She carried a brimming pail in the direction Mrs. Byrdsong had gone. Amid the confusion, Cassie continued offering water to the wounded throughout the long day.

The sun was low on the horizon when Mrs. Byrdsong brought her a mangled piece of bread. "Thank you," Cassie said, devouring it in four bites.

Just as she finished eating, two shots from the enemy's battery hit a ship in the river. The realization they weren't safe from cannon fire, even under the high riverbanks of the York, made her retch, losing the precious bread she had eaten too hurriedly.

Mrs. Byrdsong handed her a cup of water. "It's the *Charon.* Lord, help us. What will be next?"

A man rushed up to Cassie. "I need your bucket." He grabbed the bucket and ran toward the riverbank.

Cassie and Mrs. Byrdsong watched as the men attempted to douse the flames. In spite of their efforts, the ship became engulfed with fire. The crew and the firefighters made a hasty escape to the shore.

Cassie rushed to the water's edge, determined to retrieve her bucket. She stood for a moment, watching flames shoot into the night. The flames, along with the cannon fire, filled the waterfront with a strange orange light. Seeing the burning ship, Cassie worried the British were losing the battle. If that happened, she would be back at Blanton Hall. She was every bit as trapped here as she had been there. She still had no choices, except to keep on doing what Mrs. Byrdsong told her to do.

Pushing aside her fears, Cassie looked around for the man who had taken her bucket, but she didn't see him. She spotted three abandoned buckets where the ship's crew and firefighters left them after coming ashore. She picked up a bucket and returned to help Mrs. Byrdsong.

19
Between the Lines

The following morning Cassie awoke where she had collapsed beside her water bucket. She had slept only intermittently. The belching cannonade and shaking earth woke her from time to time, and only her complete exhaustion enabled her to get back to sleep. Now as she looked around, she saw that the constant bombardment was taking its toll on Yorktown. The British were losing the battle. In all likelihood when the fighting was over, she'd be returned to slavery. Shaking dirt from her petticoat, Cassie filled her bucket and went to find Mrs. Byrdsong.

Mrs. Byrdsong was on her knees, washing grime from an injured soldier's face. She, who had seemed untiring during early hours of the bombardment, now looked tired and spent.

"Where should I start?" Cassie asked.

Mrs. Byrdsong looked up and her eyes were sad. "I need to talk with you as soon as I'm done here." She finished with the soldier, stood, and led Cassie away from the wounded. "It breaks my heart to have to tell you that all the escaped slaves are being expelled from Yorktown." Tears rose in her eyes and she looked away. "We've no longer enough food to feed everyone."

Cassie couldn't believe she had heard correctly. "B-But . . . there're thousands of us."

Mrs. Byrdsong shook her head and wiped furiously at her eyes with her filthy apron. "I know. It's not right. It's just not right."

Cassie reeled and could hardly speak. "What will happen to us?"

Mrs. Byrdsong swallowed hard. "You'll be put out between the lines."

Cassie's eyes filled. "But there's a b-battle going on."

"Sending out the smallpox victims was terrible, but that was before the battle began. This is worse. If you make it safely through the lines, then those awful slave patrols will be after you."

Cassie still was having trouble accepting this terrifying news. "I thought you said Cornwallis was sure to win."

"He always has won. However, before he wasn't fighting the Continentals and the French artillery experts." Mrs. Byrdsong reached out and put an arm around Cassie. "You'd better sit down. You look right peaked."

Cassie slumped onto the grass. Jumbled thoughts filled her mind. The British had betrayed her, just like the Nicholses. It didn't matter that she'd work hard for them. How could this be happening?

"You stay right here until I come back." Mrs. Byrdsong wrung her hands. "I'm going to see if I can round you up a few things."

Cassie felt like saying it was pointless for Mrs. Byrdsong to bother since there was little hope for her. But saying anything seemed too great an effort.

It wasn't long before Mrs. Byrdsong returned. "I found you a clean blanket. The nights are cold, and . . ." Her voice trailed off. She sighed deeply. "And here's some Indian corn; that's all they're giving to former slaves." Mrs. Byrdsong unhooked her scissors from her belt. "Take these, too."

"B-B-But you'll need these for the b-bandages."

"I'll get another pair. Scissors make a good weapon. If you need to, use them to defend yourself."

Forcing down the fear that rose in her throat, Cassie swallowed hard. "A weapon?"

"They'll only be a weapon if you are set upon. I didn't get a wink of sleep last night, thinking over what you must do. Never let on you're a runaway slave. No one can tell by looking at you," Mrs. Byrdsong warned. "You must say your name's Cassandra. Cassie sounds like a slave name. If anyone wants to know your business, tell them you are an assistant hairdresser, plying your trade among the camp followers. Show them the scissors as proof. Here, take a comb too. You won't be lying, only stretching the truth a bit. Anyway, a preacher told me once that lying was acceptable if you did so to save your life or someone else's."

"How can I l-lie? Because I stutter, people don't believe me even when I tell the truth."

"Give it your best effort. If you're caught, from what you've told me, you'll be flogged within an inch of your life."

Mrs. Byrdsong was giving her good advice. Yet Cassie wondered how she would ever be able to pass for white and to lie with her stutter, even to save her life.

The initial shock of Mrs. Byrdsong's announcement passed and Cassie began to think about her situation. It might be unrealistic, but maybe she could avoid the slave hunters and make her way to Williamsburg and Aunt Ida and Moses. They could hide her and help her figure out what to do. Perhaps she would be able to find her father.

"Come along," Mrs. Byrdsong said. "I'll stay with you as long as I can."

They walked side by side to the outer defensive line. Mrs. Byrdsong's steps were slow and her shoulders stooped as if she were carrying a huge basket on her back. The closer they came to the no-man's land that divided the two armies, the louder grew the roar of cannon. The smell of powder filled the air, and the ground shook when a shell landed nearby.

British soldiers urged a struggling mass of former slaves forward. Cassie's tears overflowed as she saw what lay ahead. Mrs. Byrdsong put both arms around her. "There, there, you'll not be alone. My thoughts and prayers will be with you." This sounded to Cassie so much like what Aunt Ida had told her that last night in Williamsburg she swallowed her sobs and wiped her eyes.

"You've been awfully good to me. Thank you for everything."

Mrs. Byrdsong smiled sadly at her. "You're a good girl." Again, Cassie was struck by the memory that Aunt Ida had said similar words to her. "I'll miss you, Cassie."

Mrs. Byrdsong drew away, sniffling. She folded the blanket she had found for Cassie. "Let me fasten this across your chest." She took out a cord and with it secured the blanket under Cassie's left arm. "Let me tell you about Indian corn. You can't eat it without grinding or boiling it."

With a tremendous roar a cannonball exploded in the midst of the assembled slaves. A number fell, screaming in agony. Cassie put a hand over her mouth and turned her eyes away. In the dim light, she saw Mrs. Byrdsong's face had turned as white as her mobcap.

Soldiers with bayonets began prodding the slaves still standing. "You better go," Cassie said.

Mrs. Byrdsong nodded, anger and worry distorting her usually pleasant face. She went to one side as the slaves began moving. She wiped at her eyes and yelled at Cassie. "Remember what I told you!"

In the confusion, Cassie was propelled forward with the others. She searched the bystanders for Mrs. Byrdsong, finally catching a last glimpse of her before she was obscured by the mass of frightened slaves. Cassie's eyes smarted with tears. Her tears, the darkness, and the smoke from the cannon made it hard to see. But she kept going.

Cannonballs flew over her head. Off to her side, Cassie thought she saw lots of digging going on. The Continentals were building new fortifications closer to the town and paid little attention to the horde of former slaves.

They seemed to be heading across an open field to woods that appeared and then disappeared in the flashing lights from the cannon. From time to time, groups or individuals struck off by themselves in another direction. Cassie didn't know whether to stay with the others or take her chances on her own. The wrong decision might cost her life.

Musket fire erupted from the soldiers dug in on Cassie's right. A bullet whizzed by her head. She heard heartrending screams as the bullets found their marks and slaves fell. Others began to shout, "Don't shoot! Don't shoot!"

In panic, the horde of slaves turned away from the gunfire and began running in the opposite direction. Caught in the frenzy of the mob, Cassie feared falling and being trampled. She had to get away from the others. Perhaps if she could make it through the lines under the cover of darkness, tomorrow she could find her way to Williamsburg, to Aunt Ida, and Moses.

The firing stopped. The soldiers must have realized the slaves were unarmed.

Cassie's stomach churned. Now as she looked around, everywhere she looked, there were soldiers. Which way should she go?

20
The Woods

Running toward the nearest woods, Cassie skirted the wounded slaves. She heard their pitiful cries for help, but terror drove her onward. Her side hurt and she stumbled on a tree root, turning an ankle. The sharp pain made her gasp, but she kept going. She was almost at the woods when a loud command brought her to a sudden halt. "Qui va là?"

Cassie didn't recognize the language, but she understood the tone of voice. A soldier had heard or seen her. Probably one of the French soldiers. She crouched hoping if she didn't move, no one could see her. Her sides heaved and her breathing sounded as loud in her ears as the barrage overhead. Minutes passed. No one came for her.

She stood and began to run again, drawing on what was left of her depleted strength. Out of breath and sides heaving, she reached the shelter of a stand of trees and collapsed in the underbrush. Her breathing calmed and she heard voices a short distance away. This wouldn't be a safe place to stay.

Cassie struggled up and plunged deeper into the woods. The foliage obscured the light from the bombardment, making it hard to see. In her haste, she hit her head on a low-hanging branch. Reaching up, she felt wetness. Her head throbbed, but she guessed it was only a scrape.

The woods grew thicker. Cassie continued on and on, until her legs refused to go further. It was too dark to see anything properly. Kneeling she untied her blanket and with both hands scooped up the fragrant-smelling fallen leaves into a mound. Then she wrapped herself in the blanket, covering it with leaves as best as she could. She lay in the cold darkness listening to the menacing sound of the cannons, exhausted and frightened. What would tomorrow bring?

It was just beginning to get light when Cassie opened her eyes. She wasn't sure if she'd slept or not. She got up stiffly, shaking the leaves from her blanket, relieved to have survived the night without being killed or captured. Her stomach growled, reminding her it had been many hours since she had eaten. Untying the bundle with the Indian corn, she found that, in addition to the corn, Mrs. Byrdsong had given her a piece of dark, heavy bread. Cassie sank her teeth hungrily into the stale bread, ate half of it, and then carefully put the rest back in her bundle.

Woods surrounded her, but she had to find the Williamsburg road. She decided to leave the blanket Mrs. Byrdsong had given her, thinking it might make her look suspicious. Williamsburg lay to the west of Yorktown, away from the rising sun. She began picking her way carefully in that direction, listening to every sound and trying to move silently. She hadn't gone far when she stepped on a fallen branch and its loud cracking startled her.

"Arrêtez!" someone called in a commanding voice. Through the trees, she saw a soldier in a white uniform. He was a big man with a red face and he was aiming his musket directly at her.

Cassie's heart leapt to her throat. She didn't dare move.

The soldier came slowly toward her, lowering his gun as he neared. He said something rapidly in an unfamiliar language. He was probably one of the French soldiers allied with the Continental army. Mrs. Byrdsong's advice came to mind. Cassie eased the scissors and comb from her bundle and made cutting and combing motions.

The soldier laughed, showing lots of white teeth, and motioned for her to follow him.

Cassie wondered if she should turn and make a run for it. The appearance of two more soldiers in white uniforms made her realize soldiers were probably in this whole area and she had better not chance running.

They only walked for about five minutes when the woods opened into a clearing filled with tents and soldiers. The soldiers brought her to a man, most probably an officer, in an immaculate blue uniform, seated inside a tent, studying a map. He wore a white wig and highly polished boots.

The soldier who had first spotted her, saluted, and then said something rapidly to the man. The man in the blue uniform looked up, as if annoyed by the interruption. Cold blue eyes glared at Cassie and then the man spoke in perfect English. "What's your business here, girl?"

21
Mrs. Simpson

"I got l-lost," Cassie stammered, knowing her stutter made her look suspicious. At the same time, she knew she had to speak up for herself. There was no Zinnia here to stand up for her. She took a deep breath and made a great effort to control her stutter. "I'm an assistant hairdresser and I got separated from my m-mistress during the night. I got scared and I couldn't find my way b-back to the others."

The officer sighed. "I haven't time to deal with camp followers. My men will see you get headed in the direction of the Continental lines." He gave an order in the language Cassie didn't understand and with a wave of his hand dismissed her.

With a rush of hope, Cassie realized she had stood up for herself, and the officer had believed her in spite of her stutter. The soldier who had found her in the woods hustled her away. He led her through the woods to a road that ran behind the trenches and pointed in the direction she was to go.

The sun was fully up now and the day promised to be warm. Cassie headed uncertainly toward the Continental lines. The Patriots would surely turn her over to the slave patrols. Her fears intensified when she met a bedraggled group of slaves, guarded by two Continental soldiers. She didn't look at the slaves, afraid one of them might recognize her and give her away.

An empty supply wagon, drawn by six mules, lumbered toward her. Cassie was walking into the rising sun, so the wagon was headed toward Williamsburg. How she wished she dared ask the driver if she could have a ride. As the wagon drew closer, she saw that the driver was a stocky woman, wearing a home-spun jacket, a petticoat, and a man's hat. She smiled at Cassie. On an impulse, Cassie waved for the woman to stop.

"Ho," the woman called to the mules, pulling up on the reins.

"Are you going to Williamsburg?" Cassie asked.

"Very near there. Port Anne. Hop up."

Cassie climbed into the high seat, fearful of what might happen next. She wondered if she had done the right thing by hailing this woman.

The driver clucked to the mules, flicked the reins, and the wagon lurched forward. She turned toward Cassie. "I'm Mrs. Simpson."

Cassie knew she had to respond. "Cassandra B-Byrdsong."

"What's a young'un like you doing here with a battle going on?"

This was the question Cassie had been dreading. She reached in the bundle again, producing the scissors and comb. "I came to earn a few coins."

Mrs. Simpson rearranged her hat. "Well, I guess you might ask me what I am doing out here. I'll tell you. Ever since my husband was killed in the war, I've had to take over the freight-hauling business. I keep up with the army the best I can, hauling whatever they need."

"Do you l-live in Williamsburg?"

"No, I'm from Charles City County. Are you headed to Williamsburg?"

"Yes, I've seen enough fighting. I'm going home." Cassie wasn't lying. Williamsburg was the only home she had.

Mrs. Simpson seemed to consider for a moment. Cassie held her breath. "You don't talk so well, do you?"

Cassie swallowed and nodded her head. Mrs. Simpson continued. "I had a cousin who stuttered. He outgrew it. I hope you do too."

They rode on in silence passing soldiers and other recaptured slaves. Whenever she saw them, Cassie turned away. Mrs. Simpson must have noticed. "They're a sorry sight, sure enough, poor beggars."

Did this Mrs. Simpson suspect Cassie was an escaped slave? Some people had thought Cassie was white. Now she hoped Mrs. Simpson was one of them.

The mules plodded toward Williamsburg. They met a number of heavily loaded wagons, headed in the direction of Yorktown. Mrs. Simpson knew the other drovers and she called out to them by name. If any of them thought it was unusual for Mrs. Simpson to be riding with a slave, to Cassie's relief, no one said anything. In fact, she wondered if they even noticed her.

They had gone several miles when they passed the driveway that led to Blanton Hall. Cassie held her breath as they passed, praying that no one from there was out and about who would recognize her. She thought about Zinnia, hoping that even in her sickened condition, she had been able to get away. If she was back at Blanton Hall, Cassie imagined Adrianna questioning Zinnia about her. Unfortunately, any interest Adrianna had in Cassie would be for all the wrong reasons. She remembered Adrianna saying, "You belong to me." She again resolved to belong only to herself.

The farther they got from the battlefield and Blanton Hall, the more hopeful Cassie became. They rounded a curve and met a unit of Continental soldiers. Mrs. Simpson pulled off the road to let them pass. They marched to a tune Cassie recognized as "Yankee Doodle," played by their fifers and drummers. Cassie had been so used to the spit and polish of the British soldiers in the encampment the appearance of the Continentals surprised her. Many of their uniforms looked like they were homespun, and the color of their buff breeches varied from light beige to almost gold. Yet, they marched jauntily along under a flag with words on it.

"What does it say on the flag?" Cassie asked. She knew her letters and could sound out words, but the flag went by so rapidly, she couldn't figure them out.

Mrs. Simpson opened a pouch, took out a plug of chewing tobacco, and put it into her mouth. She chewed for a moment before speaking. "It says, 'Don't tread on me.' That's what this war is all about."

Cassie liked the words, but she didn't say anything. Did these soldiers, free men, really know what it was like to be tread upon?

Back on the road again, they continued on toward Williamsburg. It was late morning when at the turning for Port Anne, Mrs. Simpson pulled the mules to a stop. "This is as far as I can take you."

Cassie jumped down. "Thank you for the ride."

"Good luck, Cassandra."

With a smile, Cassie waved goodbye. So far, she had been very lucky. Mrs. Simpson had asked few questions and had seemed satisfied with Cassie's answers. If only her luck would hold.

In the distance Cassie spotted the familiar spire of Bruton Parish Church. It was too dangerous for her to go into town during the daytime. Someone might recognize her. She'd have to hide until dark. Then she would make her way to the Nicholses' house and to the safety, however temporary, of Aunt Ida's arms.

Looking around, Cassie saw a falling-down shack, probably once used to dry tobacco. She crossed a field to the derelict building. A door hung half on and half off leather hinges. It creaked as she moved it aside and went inside. The floor was littered with mouse droppings. She swept them aside with her hand, sat, and opened her bundle. Taking out the rest of the hard, dark bread, she slowly ate it. Soon she would be in the loving embraces of Aunt Ida and Moses. It had been eight long months since she had seen them. She closed her eyes and rested, filled with thoughts of home.

Shadows were lengthening when Cassie opened her eyes. She waited until it was quite dark before returning to the road and making her way into Williamsburg.

No one paid any attention to her as she walked up Francis Street to the Nicholses' house. Lights gleamed in the parlor windows, and the house looked the same as it always had. Cassie followed the familiar path around the side to the back and the quarters.

The quarters were dark. That was strange. It was too early for Aunt Ida and Moses to be abed. Cassie's heart raced as she covered the last several yards to the quarters and knocked at the door. No one answered. She went to the window and peered inside. All was darkness. Where were Aunt Ida and Moses?

"What are you doing poking around in the dark?" someone asked in a threatening voice.

22
Williamsburg

It sounded like a boy, but Cassie couldn't make out anyone in the darkness. "I'm I-looking for Aunt Ida and M-Moses."

"They're not here anymore."

Cassie peered into the shadows. She could just make out a dim figure. "Where'd they go?"

The figure came closer. It was a boy, and Cassie realized it must be the one the Nicholses' traded her for.

"Where are they?" Cassie asked again, her voice quavering with the fear that something awful had happened. "I used to I-live here."

The boy hesitated. "There's no easy way to tell you this. Aunt Ida died."

Cassie gasped. "Oh, no!"

The boy continued in an even voice. "After you left, she went to bed and wouldn't get up. Moses say she died of a broken heart."

"And M-Moses?"

"He followed soon after. He had a bad cough, lung fever. Folks say he just couldn't go on without Aunt Ida."

Cassie felt like she'd been punched in the stomach. "Dead? Aunt Ida, M-Moses dead?" Her voice broke with a sob. In the months she'd been away, two of the three people in the whole world who cared about her had died.

"I'm sorry," the boy said.

Cassie put her hand on the side of the quarters to steady herself. "No, no, it can't be." She began to sob uncontrollably.

"Hush up now before somebody hears you," the boy warned. "Come with me."

Trying to stifle the sobs that wracked her whole body, Cassie followed the boy into the garden behind the quarters. Her heart ached as if someone had stomped on it. Dear Aunt Ida and Moses were gone. Gone as surely as if the earth had opened up and swallowed them. Her legs gave out and she collapsed onto the ground, burying her head in her hands.

Cassie struggled for control, her whole body shuddering with every effort to suppress her sobs. She frantically wiped her eyes and blew her nose into her handkerchief. She would never see Aunt Ida's gentle smile again or hear Moses tell Bible stories in his deep voice. She shook her head in disbelief. "Aunt Ida and M-Moses passed and I never knew."

The boy sat nearby, speaking again only when her sobs began to lessen. "Aunt Ida told me about you. I saw you the day you left. Mens came looking for you back about three months ago, in August, I think. Where've you been since then?"

"With the B-British at Yorktown. They promised freedom to slaves who joined them. Then they drove us out."

"Where are you going now?"

Cassie sniffled and blew her nose. "I don't know. I was going to ask Aunt Ida and Moses for advice."

The boy was quiet for a moment. "I guess you could stay the night in their old quarters. No one lives there now. The Nicholses don't have anyone here but me. They hire a widow woman who comes each morning to clean and cook. I sleep on a pallet in the gun shop to keep people from thinkin' about stealin' the guns."

Cassie could go no further that night. "I'll stay."

"Have you had anything to eat?"

"Some b-bread."

"Apples in the orchard are ripe. I'll get you a few." The boy got up.

Cassie was left alone, her sadness as immeasurable and dark as the night. The boy was back a few minutes later with his shirt full of apples. He walked her back to the quarters.

"What will you do tomorrow?" the boy asked.

"Perhaps I'll b-be able to find my father." Cassie's tears began again.

"Where's he at?"

"I don't know."

At the door, the boy gave her the apples. "You best be gone at first light."

"Thank you," she said, sniffling. She went inside without even saying goodnight. The boy had been kind and she had been so distraught she had never asked his name.

The quarters were empty. What had happened to Aunt Ida's chest and the rocking chair Moses had lovingly made her? Cassie felt as empty as the room.

Climbing into the loft, she lay down on the hard planks where once she had slept on a comfortable straw mattress. She shivered, wishing she had kept the blanket Mrs. Byrdsong had given her.

Cassie had once heard someone say they were bereft. She hadn't really understood the word until now. She had lost two dear people and her refuge. Memories of Aunt Ida and Moses mixed with horrible images from the last days flooded her mind. Perhaps her father was dead too and going to look for him was a fool's errand. She desperately wished for sleep. Perhaps then the awful hurt and sadness would go away. If only she could sleep, perhaps tomorrow she could figure out what to do, where to go.

Her tears began again. As she sank deeper and deeper into her grief, Aunt Ida's voice seemed to come to her, "Our love will go with you always and forever." Cassie wrapped these words around her like a blanket and held them close through the long, restless night.

23
On the Road

A rooster crowed, waking Cassie. It was just growing light. In spite of everything, she had managed to get a few hours sleep. Aunt Ida and Moses, dead. She still found it impossible to believe. She would never see them again. A look around the deserted quarters, once so warm and welcoming, brought home to her again the dreadful truth. They were gone, gone forever.

Her stomach grumbled. She found and ate one of the apples the boy had given her. She shivered as she took the comb from her bundle and tried to neaten her hair. She retied her bundle, putting in the apples. Cassie wasn't sure where she was going, but she knew she couldn't stay in Williamsburg. If anyone in town recognized her, they would return her to Blanton Hall.

Taking a last, sorrowful look around the quarters and wiping tears from her eyes, Cassie slipped out the door and made her way to Duke of Gloucester Street, Williamsburg's main thoroughfare.

The little town was just coming awake. Smoke came from kitchens, and slaves opened shutters and blinds. People were not yet out on the streets. Cassie didn't want to go in the direction of Yorktown and Blanton Hall, so she headed toward Richmond, the town farther inland where last year the Patriots had established the new capital of Virginia. They had hoped the capital would be safe from the British. But early in 1781, the British had burned it. She didn't know what, if anything, she would find there, but it was the only direction she could take.

Passing the College of William and Mary, closed now because of the war, she hurried along until she was well outside the town. Then she slowed her pace. She was more tired than she had ever been in her life, but she had to put as much distance as she could between Williamsburg and herself.

As Cassie walked along in the crisp early morning air, she tried to think what she should tell anyone who stopped her. She had to have a story ready to explain why a girl her age was on her way to Richmond alone. But, her brain refused to work.

A wagon appeared over the top of a hill and rumbled toward her. Cassie held her breath, but the driver only nodded in her direction as he passed. Ten minutes later, two horsemen, traveling fast, came into view. They flew by Cassie without even acknowledging her presence. Her appearance didn't seem to be arousing suspicion. Her petticoat and mobcap were soiled, but her mother's handsome jacket was undamaged. She hoped she looked like an ordinary girl, a white girl.

At midmorning, a wagon came up behind her, and to her horror, the driver pulled to stop. "Would you be wanting a ride?" the driver asked.

Cassie turned to decline the offer. But as tired and heavy hearted as she was, she didn't think she should pass up a ride. She studied the man in the wagon. He was an old fellow with a wrinkled face, pendulous, unshaven jowls and cloudy eyes. Perhaps he wouldn't look too closely at her. Perhaps he wouldn't guess she was an escaped slave. "Thank you," Cassie said. "I'd appreciate a ride."

"Hop in the back."

Cassie climbed into the wagon and found a place to sit on top of a stack of lumber. "Where're you headed?" the man asked.

She spit out the word. "Richmond."

"You haven't run away from home, have you?"

Cassie thought fast, but tried to speak with precision, avoiding the letters that made her stutter. "I'm headed to Richmond. I'm a hairdressing assistant and I've been offered work there."

The man grunted. "I can take you only as far as Providence Forge."

"That will be a b-big help." Cassie sighed deeply. So far, so good.

The wagon rumbled over the rutted road. The lumber was hard, but Cassie was grateful to be off her feet and where the man couldn't look at her without turning around. They rode in silence for the nearly two hours or so that it took to reach the hamlet of Providence Forge.

Thanking the man, Cassie got down from the wagon. The man tipped his hat in acknowledgement.

Three horses were tied to hitching posts in front of an ordinary. Apparently, other travelers had stopped for a meal. The man pulled his wagon off the road, got down, and without a glance in Cassie's direction went inside.

Her empty stomach growled, but she had never eaten in such a place. She took out her pocket, went to the back of the ordinary, and knocked on the door. A woman in a headscarf with blue-black skin came to the door. Cassie let down her guard ever so slightly. "Please, could I b-buy a l-loaf of b-bread?" she pleaded, jingling the coins in her pocket.

The woman looked questioningly at her and then at the pocket. "Stay here," she said.

Minutes passed. If the woman had gone for bread, she was gone a long time. What if she was alerting the owner of the ordinary that the girl at the back door was a runaway? As hungry as she was, Cassie decided she couldn't take a chance. She turned and fled.

Not daring to return to the road, Cassie ran into the woods, not stopping until she was well away from the ordinary. Minutes had passed and no one raised the hue and cry that would mean someone was looking for her. Forcing herself to stop, she tried to get her bearings. If she traveled parallel to the Richmond road, she could return to it when she was sure no one was following her.

Cassie threaded her way through the thick woods, trying to keep the road within sight. She stumbled over a tree branch and almost fell. From time to time, she spotted the road through the thick undergrowth. Seeing it reassured her she was not lost.

Weak from grief, fear, and hunger, Cassie pulled a handful of Indian corn from her bundle and put it in her mouth. She held the hard and unyielding corn in her mouth several minutes before spitting it out. Next she tried one of the sour apples. Her stomach cramped, but she kept walking.

Suddenly, she stepped into a small animal hole, lost her balance, and fell. She cried out in surprise and pain. Moments later, realizing she wasn't hurt, she got up and struggled on.

Hearing the gurgle and splash of running water, Cassie headed toward the sound. Her mouth was as dry as hay stored in a barn. A small run snaked through a ravine. She half slid, half ran down the bank to the water.

Lying down, she drank the cold water gratefully, its refreshing coolness quenching her thirst. She ate another apple and stretched out on the mossy bank beside the stream. How could she go on without food, without friends? The dream of finding her father was just that, a dream. He might be dead, like dear, dear Aunt Ida and Moses. She could die here in the woods and no one would ever know. Tears rolled down her cheeks. She cried and cried until she fell asleep.

A twig snapped. Cassie awoke with a start. Night was falling and the woods were already growing dark. Someone or something was near. She got up noiselessly, listening intently. She held her breath, regretting she had fallen asleep.

24

The Puppeteers

"Hello?" someone said in a pleasant voice. "Is anyone there?"

Cassie didn't know whether to run or to answer. If she did run, she wasn't sure which direction to run in, so she answered, "It's only m-me."

Another twig cracked and she heard steps approaching. In the dim light, she could just make out a white boy about her size.

"What are you doing out here?" he asked in the same non-threatening voice.

Cassie wasn't sure how to answer. "I wanted a drink of water and I fell asleep. I think I've b-become l-lost."

"Well, it's getting dark. You best follow me to our camp." The boy was carrying a pail of water. He turned and headed off.

Cassie didn't know what to do. Her heart was beating fast. She could run in the opposite direction. But it would soon be completely dark.

The boy stopped and turned. "Come along. Nobody will hurt you."

Cassie hesitated another moment and then followed the boy. He led her to the top of the ravine and from there to a clearing. A woman, wearing a hat with a feather and long, dangling earrings, stirred a pot that rested in the coals of a fire. She wore a beaded jacket and a striped petticoat. A swarthy man with a deeply lined face, an earring in one ear, and a large, drooping mustache

104

lounged near the fire. He wore a red shirt with a patterned kerchief knotted at the neck.

In the flickering firelight, Cassie noticed a wagon nearby that looked like a little house on wheels. She could just make out a red and white painting on the side, but it was too dark to see it clearly.

"I found this girl down by the stream," the boy said. "She's lost." He stepped closer to the fire and Cassie saw he was also wearing a red shirt and a patterned kerchief.

"Come, sit, and share our meal," the woman said, indicating a log pulled up near the fire. "Then you can tell us what you're doing out at night in the middle of nowhere."

The meaty smell of whatever was cooking in the pot made Cassie's stomach growl. She sat and the woman passed her a bowl of stew and a spoon. Cassie didn't want to appear starved, but the rich smell was overpowering. She dug into the bowl with her spoon, eating hungrily, only stopping when she became conscious the others were looking at her.

"You were hungry," the woman said. "Give me your bowl, there's plenty more."

Cassie noticed the woman's hands. Her fingers were thick and knotted and she handled the bowl awkwardly. Cassie ate the second bowl more slowly. When she was done, the woman said. "I am Madame Golinda. This is my brother Jacko and you have already met Peter, my son. Now, young lady, tell us who you are and how you happen to be lost."

With her stomach full, Cassie recovered a little. She took a deep breath. "I'm Cassandra B-Byrdsong," she said, trying to sound confident and stutter as little as possible. "I was going to stay with Aunt Ida and M-Moses in Williamsburg, but they b-both died." Cassie's eyes filled and she wiped at the tears with her hand. "I'm on the way to try and find my father. I was walking and got thirsty and tired. I fell asleep and when I woke, it was growing dark."

"Where's your father?" Madame Golinda asked.

Cassie hesitated, her thoughts tumbling in her head. She had better be cautious. "I'm not sure. I think he's in New York."

The man called Jacko spoke up, "New York? How does a young girl like you plan to get to New York?"

Cassie shook her head. "I don't know. B-But he's my only family."

"How do you plan to pay for your journey?" Madame Golinda asked.

"I'm trained as a hairdresser."

Madame Golinda's eyes grew sharp like a hawk. "Are you a runaway indentured servant?"

At the word *runaway*, Cassie's heart leapt, but the next words, *indentured servant*, reassured her. Madame Golinda must think she was white. Cassie shook her head decisively. As before, she tried to be as truthful as possible. "No, m-ma'am, I learned hairdressing from M-Mary, an indentured servant, but I've never been indentured."

Madame Golinda seemed to consider for a moment. "We're headed to Richmond tomorrow. You best tag along with us so that you don't get lost again. We are to bed soon and up with the light."

When the meal was finished, Madame Golinda loaned Cassie a heavy blanket and indicated she should lie down near the wagon. Cassie stretched out under the blanket, looking up at the stars so distant and lonely in the vast blackness of the night. Tears filled her eyes. She sobbed silently for Aunt Ida and Moses, for Zinnia, for the fallen at Yorktown, and for the whole weeping world. Finally, she slept.

It was already light when Cassie woke and rubbed the sleep from her swollen eyes. She wondered what she looked like and if the others could tell she had been crying. In the harsh light of day would Madame Golinda discover she wasn't white and reevaluate her offer?

Seeing her awake, Peter came to where she slept. For the first time, Cassie saw him clearly. He had olive skin, dark hair and eyes, a nose with a bump on it, and a birthmark, shaped something like a star, under his left nostril.

"Good morning, tea's ready," Peter said. "My mother makes a fine tea from berries and herbs. You'll like it."

Cassie got up and began folding the blanket. "I'd be grateful for some tea. But first, I'd l-like to wash my face and comb my hair."

Peter pointed to a bucket near the wagon. "There's still water left from last night."

Before going to the fire for tea, Cassie splashed cold water on her face and cupping her hands, held some to each eye. Then she combed her hair and adjusted her mobcap. After she was done, she studied the picture on the wagon. It was a stage with players on it. Peter saw her looking at it. "Have you ever seen a Punch and Joan show?"

Cassie shook her head. "Well, you've got a treat in store for you. Punch and Joan are puppets, and we're traveling puppeteers. Our props and puppets are in the wagon. We have a portable theater for hand puppets and a stage for our wire puppets."

"Oh," Cassie said, not fully understanding because she had never seen puppets.

"We go to Richmond, then to Fredericksburg, Annapolis, Chestertown, and Philadelphia. We'll winter in New York. In towns with theaters or taverns with a long room, we can set up the wire puppets. In small places we have shows on the street."

Cassie brightened at the mention of New York. "I'd l-like to get to New York to find my father."

"We left New York months ago, thinking there was going to be a big battle there. But instead, we ran into it down here." Peter laughed and shook his head. "We were going to Williamsburg, but when we heard about the fighting at Yorktown, we decided to head north again. New York's a grand place, almost as grand as Philadelphia."

"Peter," Madame Golinda called. "Stop talking Cassandra's ears off and give her a chance to have a cup of tea. It's time you watered and fed the horses."

Peter smiled at Cassie. "I like to talk, and I don't have any-one to talk to most of the time except for Mother and Uncle Jacko. I hope you can stand it."

Peter's warm manner put Cassie at ease. "I can't talk m-much. So, I don't m-mind l-listening."

Smiling again, Peter turned to his chores and Cassie joined Madame Golinda at the campfire. After last night's meal and more sleep, the heavy weight of Cassie's despair lifted a little. "M-May I help?" she asked.

"You can help yourself to a piece of bread." Madame Golinda passed the crusty, round loaf and a knife to Cassie. "We'll be on our way shortly."

Madame Golinda turned away and began packing the wagon. Cassie's earlier fears of discovery seemed unfounded. She cut herself a slice of the fragrant sourdough bread. She ate slowly this morning, savoring each delicious bite, wondering when and where she would eat again.

Not more than a half hour later, the puppeteers were on the road. Cassie and Peter walked beside the wagon while Madame Golinda and Jacko rode. Peter chatted happily to Cassie as they made their way toward Richmond. They met wagons, riders, and other people on foot. No one seemed to pay attention to Cassie now that she was with the puppeteers. As hours passed and they drew near to Richmond, Cassie began to dread being on her own again.

25
Richmond

The puppeteer's wagon jolted into Richmond. The sound of hammering and sawing and the smell of fresh-cut lumber came from new buildings under construction. In other places, charred ruins were a stark reminder of the destruction of war. Farm wagons and pedestrians clogged the road. They passed market stalls and stores. A number of citizens of Williamsburg had relocated to Richmond when the capital had moved there. Cassie looked around warily, fearing she'd see someone who would recognize her.

Jacko stopped before a tavern with a picture of a black horse on the sign. Cassie wished she could stay with the puppeteers, but she couldn't afford to stay in a tavern. She went over to Madame Golinda who was climbing down from the wagon, shaking out her petticoat, and stretching her legs after the long ride.

"Thank you for seeing me safely here," Cassie said.

Peter rushed over to join them. "Mother, Cassandra has never seen Punch and Joan. Could she stay with us until after our first show?"

Madame Golinda scrutinized Cassie who self-consciously shifted from one foot to the other. Madame Golinda spoke slowly as if still weighing Cassie's situation in her mind. "If she was cleaned up a bit and had on a kerchief, perhaps she could work the crowd with Jacko."

Peter clasped Cassie's hand, giving it a squeeze. "Thank you, Mother."

Cassie didn't have any idea what *working the crowd* entailed. But the very thought of being in a crowd terrified her. What if someone recognized her? She didn't want to go back to Blanton Hall and yet she wanted to stay with the puppeteers. They had been kind to her and she felt safe with them.

"We're treating ourselves to a night under a roof and you're welcome to stay with us," Madame Golinda said.

Cassie had so little experience of the world and its ways she didn't know how to respond. She was torn between her fears and her desire to stay with the puppeteers.

Peter looked at her encouragingly and shook his head yes. "Please stay."

Cassie could not help but smile at Peter's obvious enthusiasm. "I'd I-like that."

They ate dinner inside the Black Horse Tavern, and afterwards Madame Golinda arranged rooms and ordered a bath. A servant brought a large tub to the room that Cassie was sharing with Madame Golinda and two other women travelers. The servant threw a quilt over a rope, blocking off one corner of the room. After she returned with several pails of hot water, Madame Golinda went behind the quilt and bathed.

"Your turn." Madame Golinda emerged from behind the blanket, drying her hair with a cloth.

Cassie had never had a proper bath in a tub. She went behind the blanket, undressed, and gingerly got into the water. It was only lukewarm now with soap scum floating on top. Still she luxuriated in the unaccustomed warmth and scrubbed off the filth of the last week.

As she washed her blistered feet, she thought about the long walk beside the wagon with Peter. He had been so concerned when she got a stone in her shoe he had insisted she stop and remove it. Peter made her feel important, special. She had never had a friend her own age, and she wondered if that's what friendship was, making another person feel special.

Next Cassie lathered her hair in the tepid water. She had washed it in the river at Yorktown before the bombardment began. So much had happened in a few days that it seemed like months instead of weeks since she had gotten her hair clean. She thought again about Peter. He had talked a lot as they walked along together, but she hadn't minded at all. His cheerful chatter helped her forget, at least temporarily, the memories of the battle, her sadness over Aunt Ida and Moses, and her apprehensions about the future.

Madame Golinda interrupted Cassie's thoughts. "Let me have your clothes," she said from the other side of the quilt. "We'll wash them before we turn in."

Cassie passed her the soiled shift, petticoat, jacket, mobcap, and stockings. It made sense she shouldn't put on the dirty clothes she had worn for so long, but she wondered what she would wear.

Madame Golinda passed a clean shift, stockings, and a black petticoat in to her. "The stockings are Peter's. The petticoat and shift are mine," she said. "When you come out, we'll tack them up so you don't trip over them and hurt yourself. You can wear your own jacket. After we're done here, you can wash your clothes. You may have picked up body lice."

Even though she knew she didn't have any vermin crawling on her, Cassie was not offended at Madame Golinda's suggestion. Even the best people sometime had lice.

The water grew cool and Cassie got out of the bath, dried herself, and put on the clothes Madame Golinda had brought her. For the first time in days, she was clean.

"Here's a needle and thread," Madame Golinda said, giving them to Cassie. "Just tack up the skirt in half a dozen places."

Cassie bent to the task. When she finished and looked up, she saw Madame Golinda studying her. "A bright kerchief for your hair and a few beads and you'll look like one of us." Cassie wasn't sure what Madame Golinda meant. Cassie thought it had something to do with working the crowd. What had she gotten herself into?

Cassie spent an anxious night in the unfamiliar surroundings of the inn, in the room full of strange white women, trying to figure out what to do. At long last, she decided to retrieve her own clothes as soon as possible and be on her way.

The next morning, Peter and Jacko left early to pass out handbills advertising the puppet show that would take place at five o'clock. After breakfast Cassie went to the back of the Black Horse where she had hung her clothes. They were still wet! In fact, they were so wet it must have rained during the night. With a sinking heart, she realized she had no choice but to go through with Madame Golinda's plan for her.

It was late afternoon when Peter and Jacko set up the moveable theater in the street outside of the tavern. In their room, Madame Golinda tied a red-checked scarf around Cassie's head, securing it in the back under her hair. Then from her trunk, she took three strings of red, orange, and white beads, and a necklace made of shells. She put them around her neck. "There," Madame Golinda said, admiring her work. She handed Cassie a tambourine.

The tambourine jingled when Cassie took it. Although she had never seen one before, she immediately realized its purpose.

"You'll use it to walk through the crowd between acts and after the performance. You are to collect coins from the spectators," Madame Golinda explained.

Cassie blanched. She would be drawing attention to herself, the last thing she wanted to do.

Madame Golinda raised an eyebrow. "You don't mind helping us, do you?"

Cassie swallowed. "Of course not." Cassie hoped she had spoken convincingly.

"Well, then, it's time to get busy."

Cassie followed Madame Golinda outside. Leaves were beginning to fall and the day was warm. Jacko stood in front of the theater, holding his fiddle. Seeing Madame Golinda, he began to play.

A curious crowd gathered. To Cassie the crowd looked menacing. In her desire to stay with the puppeteers, she was risking everything.

26
Punch and Joan

The crowd clapped their hands in time to the lively jig Jacko played on his fiddle. Cassie felt many eyes on her as she walked beside Madame Golinda. She wished she could escape notice, but she hardly expected to, dressed as she was. In the short time she had been with the puppeteers, she had gotten used to Madame Golinda's unusual hat and colorful outfit. But Cassie was not used to dressing that way herself. Her face grew hot and she glanced around nervously, hoping that no one would recognize her. She tried to think what to do if that happened.

The puppet theater stood on long legs in front of the tavern. A rust-colored piece of linen was tacked around three sides, leaving the back open for the puppeteers. Cassie hoped the crowd was looking at it, and not at her.

Peter and Madame Golinda disappeared behind the miniature stage. A moment later, Jacko announced in a deep voice, "Ladies and Gentlemen,

Behind the scenes at a portable puppet theater (from a George Cruikshank illustration)

The Tragical Comedy or Comical Tragedy of Punch and Judy (Cambridge: Washburn and Thomas, 1925)

114

come right this way. Madame Golinda's World Famous Punch
and Joan Show is about to begin. Step right up so you will see the
whole performance."

The crowd moved closer and more people hurried to the vi-
cinity of the puppet theater. Jacko waited until the spectators
stopped jockeying for position and then spoke again. "Without
further delay, from New York City, I present Madame Golinda's
Punch and Joan Show."

The curtains on the stage opened and a big-nosed puppet
bowed three times to the audience.

Ladies and Gentlemen, pray how do you do?
If you are happy, me happy too.
Stop and hear my merry little play;
If me make you laugh, me need not make you pay.

Cassie thought she recognized Peter's voice, but she wasn't
sure. It had to be Peter, but he sounded different.

Punch continued until the curtain closed. Then he sang off
stage until the curtain opened again. A spotted dog joined Punch.
The dog leapt up and attached its
jaws to his big nose. Cassie and
the audience broke into laughter.
Joan came on the stage next and
Punch clobbered her repeatedly
with a stick.

Cassie had never seen anything like it. The puppets captured her imagination so fully that
when the curtain came down at
the end of the first act, she just
stood clapping with the others.
Her earlier fears had momen-
tarily vanished.

Only when a man dropped
a coin in her tambourine did

Punch (from a George
Cruikshank illustration)
*The Tragical Comedy or Comical
Tragedy of Punch and Judy* (Cambridge:
Washburn and Thomas, 1925)

Cassie remember she had work to do. She moved uncertainly among the audience, keeping her eyes down in the hope that if she kept her face hidden, no one would recognize her. Coin after coin clinked into the tambourine. Cassie murmured a thank you to each contributor.

By the end of the performance, Cassie looked in astonishment at the coins in her tambourine, remembering the much-treasured shillings Moses had given her. The audience began to disperse, seemingly much more cheerful than at the beginning of the play. Cassie took a deep breath and relaxed a little. No one had recognized her.

Peter came from behind the theater, followed by Madame Golinda. Cassie gave Madame Golinda the coins. "Not bad," Madame Golinda said, looking pleased at she counted the coins. Jacko came up and handed her more coins.

"What did you think?" Peter eagerly asked Cassie.

"I I-loved it! How did you do all those characters?"

"Mother does some of them. It takes practice." Peter was obviously pleased with Cassie's delight in the show. "But it's not hard, once you learn how."

Jacko began dismantling the theater. "We've got to get the puppets put away and the theater into the wagon," Peter said, with a last look at Cassie before going off to help Jacko.

Cassie stood uncertainly by Madame Golinda. "It went well today," Madame Golinda said. "We have one more show tomorrow. You might as well stay with us through the next performance."

"Thank you," Cassie said. She had been lucky today, but would her luck hold?

The next morning her clothes were dry, but Cassie had liked yesterday's show so much, she decided to chance one more performance. The second puppet show was very like the first. She was still worried she might be recognized, but again no one seemed to pay any special attention to her.

Afterwards, Cassie changed out of the clothes Madame Golinda had lent her and put on her own again. It had been very strange. It was as if she were a different person when she wore the colorful scarf and the beads. For a short while, she had put aside her grim memories and her heartache. It had been good not to be Cassie anymore, but Cassandra, part of a troop of puppeteers. She would soon be on her own again, but she didn't want to leave without saying goodbye, without thanking the puppeteers.

Cassie found Madame Golinda outside the tavern. "Here are your things." Cassie handed Madame Golinda her shift, petticoat, scarf, and beads. "I can't thank you, Jacko, and Peter enough." Cassie turned to where Jacko and Peter were stowing gear in the wagon. "I'll never forget your kindness."

Peter stopped what he was doing and joined his mother and Cassie. "Remember what we discussed yesterday, Mother," he said. "Did you think about Cassandra staying on with us?"

"Peter wants you to stay with us," Madame Golinda said. "Ever since his sister got married and settled down, I've had to help with the puppets when we perform. And as you may have noticed, my hands have the rheumatism." Madame Golinda held out her hands with their badly swollen knuckles. "It's torture for me to make the puppets go through their paces during the performances. Peter thinks you could learn to do it."

Cassie shot Peter a grateful look. "I appreciate your confidence. B-But if I could learn to pull the strings, I could never say the words without stuttering."

"I told Peter I'd think on it, and I have. If you want to stay with us, I'll give you until we get to Annapolis. If you master the craft by then, you can come with us all the way to New York."

Cassie couldn't keep from smiling. Continuing to perform in public carried with it the risk someone might recognize her. Yet she didn't want to leave the safety of traveling with the puppeteers. "I'll try very hard to do well," she said, wondering as she spoke if she could master her stuttering enough to perform, wondering if she was making a terrible mistake.

27
Learning Puppetry

They arrived in Fredericksburg several days later to find the streets full of people. Working men had come out of their shops in aprons and stood chatting with passersby. Small children raced about, and their mothers, busily talking, paid them little attention. In front of the Three Feathers Tavern a man, wearing the blue coat and buff pants of a Continental soldier, raised a mug and yelled out a toast. "To General Washington!" A group of men on the tavern's porch raised mugs and drank to the general.

"What's going on?" Peter asked his mother.

"I'm not sure," Madame Golinda said. "I hope people are celebrating because the Continental army has won. Whatever is going on, it probably will be good for business. Peter, go and find out."

Peter walked away from the wagon to talk to two boys sitting on a nearby fence. When he returned, he announced with a wide smile, "The British have surrendered at Yorktown. The Patriots have won!" He took off his cocked hat, threw it in the air, and expertly caught it again. "They've taken thousands of prisoners. Everybody's saying the war will soon be over."

"Huzzah!" Jacko said. "A new day is coming!"

"I'm relieved," Madame Golinda chimed in. "The war hasn't been good for performers."

Cassie didn't know what the Patriots' victory at Yorktown would mean for her because they supported slavery. Yet, she feared the worst. The horrible suffering of the wounded at Yorktown flashed through her mind. At least the awful battle was over. She hoped Mrs. Byrdsong, her husband, and her son had survived.

"We play tonight in a real theater," Madame Golinda said. "We best be getting ready. I'm sure it'll go well with everyone in such a fine mood."

That evening, Cassie didn't have to collect money since the crowd paid to attend. She entered the darkened theater, lit only by lanterns on the stage, and sat with the audience. For a change, she wasn't worried about being recognized. They were a long way from Blanton Hall, and she didn't have to draw attention to herself with the tambourine.

The boisterous crowd roared when the curtain opened and Peter and Madame Golinda manipulated the wire puppets on stage. Cassie had seen the eighteen-inch, wooden puppets with moveable joints, papier-mâché faces, and wires attached to keep them upright. But she had never seen a performance in a theater before. It was magical.

Before she knew it, the show ended to cheers and huzzahs from the audience. The crowd dispersed, with much hilarity. Many were heading to a nearby tavern to celebrate General Washington's victory. Cassie waited for the puppeteers to emerge from behind the stage.

From the pleased look on Madame Golinda's face, Cassie gathered that the puppeteers' share of the proceeds would be considerable.

"I'll help you put things away," she said.

"We'll have another successful performance tomorrow," Madame Golinda said. "Winning at Yorktown has loosened everyone's purse strings." She counted coins with obvious glee before putting them in the large pocket she always wore beneath her petticoat.

Everyone, except Cassie, seemed caught up in the general good feeling brought about by the Patriot victory. Sadness weighed upon her like a heavy yoke. The British had disappointed her at Yorktown, but the victory of the Patriots increased the likelihood she'd be returned to slavery. She had no one, except the puppeteers, and it wasn't certain she could stay with them.

The day after their last performance, they traveled northward again, stopping at small towns for outdoor performances. In the evenings after his chores, Peter worked with Cassie, teaching her to be a puppeteer.

"You've got the movements down," he said one evening after a long day on the road. "And you have learned the script. Do you think you could perform without stuttering? I've noticed you don't stutter hardly at all when you are Joan, Toby, or Scaramouch."

"I've noticed too. It may be b-because I b-become them, and I'm not me. Whenever I think about it though, I b-become me again and I stutter."

"Let's run through a whole performance. We'll set up the portable theater. Maybe if you're behind it where no one can see you, maybe you won't stutter."

"I'll try it. B-But don't be disappointed if I can't do it."

"You don't think much of yourself, do you? Ever since Mother brought up the possibility of you becoming one of us, you've been saying you can't do it."

Cassie pondered Peter's words. She longed to say that if he had lived his life as a slave, he wouldn't think much of himself either. But she knew she couldn't say that. Being a slave was only an excuse. Tears sprung to her eyes. She had loved learning the script and the antics of the puppets from Peter. It reminded her of her time imagining with Adrianna, although it was much, much better. "I'll try harder," she said, sniffling a little.

"I'm sorry I made you cry. I just like having you with us."

"I like b-being with you, too." Peter had no idea how safe she felt with the puppeteers. She didn't know if she'd ever find her father, and without him, she had no one, except them.

Peter continued, "I don't know how I know, but I'm sure you can stop stuttering. You don't do it all the time. I've paid attention.

You're stuttering a lot less than when you first joined us. That means there is nothing wrong with your tongue or voice. It seems you only stutter badly when you are upset or someone is pressing you. Since you have learned the play thoroughly, it should give you no problems."

Cassie smiled. "How can I fail with you to champion me?" She appreciated Peter's faith in her, but feared she would let him down.

Peter asked Uncle Jacko to help him set up the portable theater. "So we're going to have a show," Jacko said, with a wink.

"We'll be in Annapolis in another week or so," Peter explained. "And I need to run through the play a few times with Cassie before then."

"Shall I take out my fiddle?" Jacko asked.

"Not yet." Peter gave Cassie a warm look. "Cassie's almost ready for her theater debut, but not quite. We want to run through it a couple of times without an audience."

Jacko looked disappointed, but he helped Peter set up the theater on the other side of the wagon.

A few minutes later, everything was ready. Cassie stood behind the theater with Peter at her side. He pretended he was his Uncle Jacko, introducing the play. Then as Punch Peter ventured on stage. Cassie's first part was the dog Toby. Fortunately, Toby didn't speak. All Cassie had to do was bark furiously a few times.

Next was Joan's turn to come on stage. Cassie heard Punch's call, "Joan! Joan come here this instant!"

Cassie angled Joan onto the stage and tried to speak. The words caught in her mouth. It was as if she were trying to walk down a road and came to a road block. She panicked. "I can't do it! I can't do it!"

28
Trial in Annapolis

Every night Peter and Cassie practiced and little by little her stuttering was improving, but was it enough to perform in front of an audience? It seemed the harder she tried, the more difficulty she had speaking.

"I know the script so well," Cassie said one evening, "I could say it in my sleep."

Peter gave her a reassuring smile. "Tonight we'll try it in front of Jacko and Mother."

With so much at stake, Cassie's felt butterflies in her stomach as she helped Peter set up the small puppet theater.

When they were ready, Jacko took out his fiddle. He caught Cassie's eye and smiled. Then he played a lively tune, followed by his usual announcements as if this were a regular performance.

Peter opened the curtain. Punch bowed and Peter said his lines. Cassie dried her sweaty hands on a handkerchief and concentrated, searching deep within for confidence. She wasn't sure what happened, but when her turn came, she swung into Joan's part as smoothly as if she had never stuttered a day in her life.

When the performance was over, Jacko and Madame Golinda clapped loudly. Cassie emerged from behind the theater, flush and triumphant. Peter took her hand and they bowed to their audience. "Huzzah!" Jacko called, raising both fists in the air.

Madame Golinda smiled broadly and exclaimed. "Well done!"

"Cassandra can stay with us now, can't she?" Peter asked.

Madame Golinda's face grew serious. "Puppetry isn't a game. It's a business. If Cassie does as well in Annapolis as she did tonight, she can stay."

Cassie's elation of a few minutes before disappeared at Madame Golinda's harsh-sounding words. Peter looked crestfallen. Perhaps Madame Golinda was preparing him for possible disappointment.

As Cassie helped put away the theater, she came to terms with Madame Golinda's words. She resolved to justify Peter's faith in her, to stay with the puppeteers until they reached far-away New York.

The following day was exceptionally warm for November. Maple and gum trees blazed with bright colors as they made their way through Maryland. In the afternoon they arrived at two handsome gatehouses that marked the edge of Annapolis and passed through them into the city.

The puppeteers' wagon rumbled along narrow, winding streets, Peter and Cassie walking by its side. Annapolis was larger than Williamsburg with hundreds of houses, many of them made of brick, and numerous shops. The streets were crowded with other wagons and shoppers. They passed an impressive building under construction. Peter pointed to it. "Annapolis is the capital of Maryland. That's the new capitol building."

Just beyond the new building they caught sight of the harbor, filled with tall ships and many smaller craft. By the time they stopped in front of the red brick Middleton Tavern, not far from the busy harbor, doubts filled Cassie's mind. How had she ever thought she'd be able to perform before strangers in a large city? Fortunately, she wouldn't have long to wait for her test. Madame Golinda had booked the theater beforehand, and they were performing at five o'clock.

Many people were out of doors enjoying the fine weather, and by half past four, the crowd that began to gather in front of the theater was larger than usual. In spite of the many doubts troubling her, Cassie reviewed in her mind all she had been through in the last months. She had been stronger than she could have ever imagined. I can do it. I can do it, she said over and over to herself as she watched Jacko and Peter set up the elaborate, indoor puppet theater.

Cassie took deep breaths, trying to calm her fear. Although she had been afraid many times in the last months, this fear didn't come from others who might hurt her, but rather that she might fail. Her hands were clammy and her stomach roiled.

The time came for the performance. Jacko signaled Cassie and Peter and they went to their places behind the puppet theater. The audience grew silent as Jacko began his introduction. A minute later, Peter brought Punch on stage. Joan was off stage. Punch called out, "Joan, Joan, can't you answer, my dear?"

Cassie's moment had come. She took a deep breath and answered loud and clear. "Well, what do you want, Mr. Punch?"

Puppet theater performance (from
an illustration of Robert Cruikshank)

*The Tragical Comedy or Comical Tragedy of Punch
and Judy* (Cambridge: Washburn and Thomas, 1925)

Mr. Punch replied, "Come upstairs. I want you."

Cassie usually stuttered on words beginning with *m* and *b* and her next line could determine her fate. She swallowed, before speaking in Joan's voice. "Then want must be your master. I'm busy." Her heart leapt. She said the whole line without a single stutter.

The play progressed, and Cassie, as Joan, became more and more confident. With hardly a thought, she changed from Joan to the blind man, then the doctor, and finally she became the devil who fought Punch in the final act.

The curtain closed for the end of the play, and the crowd roared their approval. Peter spontaneously gave her a big hug. "I knew you could do it!" he yelled, amid the cheering of the crowd.

Madame Golinda, looking pleased, approached her as the crowd was dispersing.

"You've done well," Madame Golinda said, shaking the coins in her purse. She took out two pennies and gave them to Cassie and Peter. "We'll have roast beef for supper. Until then, get yourself a sweet."

"I know just where to go." Peter grabbed Cassie's hand. "Come along. We'll have to hurry to get there before the shops close."

Cassie's feet seemed to be carrying her up off the ground as she and Peter left the theater. Peter led her to a big shop two blocks from the theater. "I recommend the rock candy," he said. "It lasts the longest."

Cassie thought about the shopping she had done for Mrs. Nichols. But this would be the first time she would go to a store to buy something for herself.

In the store, Peter didn't even study the several jars of candy. "I'll have a rock candy," he told the baldheaded clerk.

"I'd like the same," Cassie said. Only later, she realized she had ordered the candy without stuttering. She knew the curse of her stuttering wasn't so easily overcome. But as she sat outside on the steps eating the sugary treat, she knew she had her old enemy on the run.

They finished their treat and headed back to the theater. Out of a side street four boys appeared and sidled up to them. They looked about Peter's age, but two of them were bigger than Peter and husky.

One of the big boys demanded, "Where are you Egyptians going?" Cassie noticed he had one snaggletooth that made him look a bit like a wolf.

Peter didn't say a word. He just tried to walk away. Cassie stayed close at his side.

The bully didn't let up on Peter. "I asked a question."

Peter took Cassie's arm.

"Isn't that lovely?" another boy said. "He's protecting the Egyptian girl."

"He's hiding behind her skirts," taunted the boy who had spoken first.

Peter steered her off to one side of the street and with fists swinging attacked the first boy. He hit the surprised bully in the jaw and then turned to face the three others. "Peter!" she called, admiring his courage, but fearing for his safety. All four boys closed in around Peter and began pounding him. He stumbled under the force of their blows and fell to the pavement. Cassie looked around frantically for help.

A man wearing the buckskins of a mountaineer strode forward. He pushed the biggest boy out of the way and then grabbed two of the boys by their jackets. "Four against one isn't fair where I come from." He held the two boys at arm's length and shook them. Then he gave them a shove. Faced with the strong mountaineer, the four boys backed off, turned, and ran.

"Are you all right?" the man asked Peter, who was bleeding from the nose.

Cassie gave Peter her handkerchief and he blotted his nose. "Yes, thank you for your help."

"Think nothing of it. Fair's fair, and those boys weren't fightin' fair." He raised his hand to his hat, tipped it to Cassie, and continued on his way.

"What's an Egyptian?" she asked.

"Sometimes people confuse puppeteers with Gypsies. They call them Egyptians."

"What's wrong with Gypsies?"

"They're like Negroes. They lie and steal. They can't be trusted."

Cassie's elation at her triumph on stage vanished with Peter's remark. She wanted to tell him he was wrong, that Negroes didn't lie and steal. And yet her whole life with the puppeteers had been a lie. They thought she was white and she had been afraid to tell them the truth. The way was clear for her to go with the puppeteers to New York. Yet, if she did find her father, then they would know everything, and surely Peter would hate her for deceiving them.

29
Philadelphia

After Annapolis, the puppeteers performed in Philadelphia, the capital of the new nation. "You have been doing very well," Peter told Cassie as they finished helping Jacko pack up after their second successful performance at Philadelphia's Southwark Theater.

Punch and Joan (from a *George Cruikshank* illustration)

The Tragical Comedy or Comical Tragedy of Punch and Judy (Cambridge: Washburn and Thomas, 1925)

The sun had gone down behind the brick buildings in the nearby square and the air was chilly. Cassie pulled the multi-colored shawl Madame Golinda had lent her closer and smiled. She had done well and didn't fully understand it. She still stuttered when she spoke, but never during performances. And she got better and better at manipulating the puppets and dramatizing their story.

"Is New York l-like Philadelphia?" Cassie asked Peter when the last puppet had been put away.

"New York isn't as big as Philadelphia, and it's different. But you'll like it."

In the last months, Cassie had seen so much death, she feared her father had been killed or died from disease. "What if I can't find my father there?"

"You'll always have a place with us," Peter said, smiling. "We'll winter in New York and head back to Virginia in the spring."

Cassie frowned. She could never chance returning to Virginia.

"Cheer up," Peter said. "I'm sure you'll find your father in New York."

She gave Peter a wistful smile. How she treasured his friendship. He had encouraged her to learn puppetry and overcome her stuttering. His pleasant chatter had helped to divert her from her painful past and her fears for the future.

A block from the Wainwright Tavern, they heard yelling and heavy boots on the cobblestone street. In the dim light, Cassie saw a tall African man running, with his hands tied behind him. She stiffened. Peter took her hand and led her into the shadows. Three men and a couple of boys were close behind the African and overtook him. Two men grabbed him, threw him roughly on the ground and began kicking him.

"Come on, Cassie," Peter whispered. "Mother and Jacko will be waiting for us to join them for dinner."

Cassie didn't move. She wasn't able to tear herself away from watching the crumpled form of the slave being kicked like a dog.

The third man, wearing all black, flung himself at the two standing men. "Stop it!" he yelled. "You've recaptured him. You've no reason to beat him, too."

The men stopped kicking the African. "We don't like Quakers butting into our affairs," one of the men replied in an angry tone.

Peter pulled Cassie away from the horrible scene. "It's only an escaped slave," he said.

"W-What will happen to the man?"

"He'll probably be returned to his owner, that's all."

"L-Life with his owner couldn't have been good, or he wouldn't have run off."

"Most slaves don't know how good they have it. They are clothed and fed and have someone to look out for them."

Cassie's heart sank. Peter would never understand. How could someone who had always been free understand how terrible it was to be a slave?

The rest of the Philadelphia performances passed in a blur for Cassie. She kept thinking about the recaptured slave and Peter's remarks. If he noticed there was something wrong, he didn't say anything. She kept debating what she should do. Perhaps she should leave now, just disappear. That way Peter would never find out she was an escaped slave. But the thought of being on her own again and trying to get to New York by herself was frightening. She finally decided to leave the puppeteers as soon as they arrived in New York. It would take them at least another month to reach there. Perhaps by then she'd be able to figure out what to do if she couldn't find her father.

30
Snowstorm

The puppeteers performed in Trenton, Morristown, and Princeton as they made their way toward New York. As November progressed, the weather grew colder, and on very cold days, their audiences were meager. They stopped giving outdoor performances, and even during the indoor performances, Cassie's fingers grew so cold she found it hard to manipulate the puppets.

A snowstorm in early December caught them on the road between Morristown and New York. Cassie shivered as she walked beside Peter. She had seen snow in Williamsburg, but it had never been like this. The snow quickly covered the ground and it was almost impossible to see the road ahead. Snow clung to Cassie's petticoat, scarf, and the heavy shawl Madame Golinda had loaned her, and her shoes grew wetter with each step.

"We'll have to find a place to stop," Jacko called to them. "There should be an ordinary in a mile or so."

They trudged on until finally, they rounded a bend and saw the ordinary, a rambling place in poor repair. Its faded white paint looked gray against the dazzling white of the newly fallen snow. Although it was only the middle of the afternoon, they stopped for the night.

While Jacko and Peter saw to the horses and wagon, Cassie and Madame Golinda went inside. The ordinary was smoky, crowded, and smelled like wet wool. Seeing the half-frozen woman and girl, the men nearest the fireplace moved aside. Cassie and Madame Golinda gratefully moved close to the roaring fire.

"Two hot buttered rums," Madame Golinda told the serving girl who didn't look much older than Cassie, "and two hot ciders."

Just as the drinks arrived, Peter and Jacko came in from the barn and joined them at the fireside. Cassie sipped her hot cider, feeling the wonderful warmth dispel the chill that seemed to have seeped into her bones.

A man with a patch over one eye moved toward them. He wore the neat, serviceable knee breeches and the wool jacket of a tradesman. "Miss, don't I know you from somewhere?" he asked Cassie.

She looked at him, wondering if he was someone from Williamsburg or who had visited Blanton Hall. Panic rose in her as she tried to recall the man's face. "I don't think so."

The man scratched his head, trying to remember. "Where are you from?"

Before she could answer, Peter spoke up. "She's with us. We're traveling puppeteers. You have probably seen her in any one of the many towns we visited in the last month."

Cassie hoped that Peter had put the man off. The man shook his head. "No, it was months ago. It'll come to me." The man moved away, shaking his head.

A trickle of cold sweat ran down Cassie's back. She didn't know the man, but he obviously knew her from somewhere. It was only a matter of time before he remembered where he had seen her and exposed her to the others. When she had first joined the puppeteers, she had worried continually that someone would recognize her. As they traveled farther and farther from Williamsburg, she had become less anxious. Now what she had long dreaded had happened. She wished she could disappear into the woodwork like a tiny mouse.

A stagecoach full of travelers pulled up at the ordinary, and moments later, six new refugees from the storm came inside, stamping snow off their feet and moving toward the fire. Madame Golinda and Cassie rose from the fireside bench where they had been seated and gave their place to two older women. "We need to change out of our wet clothes," Madame Golinda said as they moved to the back of the room.

Cassie stood uneasily by Peter as Madame Golinda met with the owner of the ordinary to arrange for their stay. The owner, a burly man wearing a dirty apron, was in the taproom serving drinks to the many stranded travelers. He came from behind the bar to talk with Madame Golinda.

Cassie glanced around. The man with one eye sat at a table with three other men, playing cards. He looked up and for a moment stared at her. She shrunk back into the shadows.

"What's the matter?" Peter asked.

She didn't know what to reply. Was he suspicious? "I'm all right, nothing a change of clothes won't fix."

"Because of the storm," the ordinary owner said to Madame Golinda, "you'll have to share a bed with two other women, and the girl will have to manage with a pallet on the floor. The men will have to make do with blankets in the taproom."

"We'll take what we can get," she replied.

Cassie and Madame Golinda followed the servant girl upstairs to a big room with stained wallpaper, containing two double beds. The room had no fireplace, and it was cold.

"Get out of those clothes," Madame Golinda said. "Put on something dry."

Cassie peeled off the wet things belonging to Madame Golinda and put on her old petticoat and her mother's jacket. "Hang your wet clothes on that hook," Madame Golinda said, arranging hers on one near it. "We'd best return to the fire."

"I think I'll stay here," Cassie said. She went to a sea chest that stood at the end of one of the beds and took out two heavy, wool blankets.

"Are you feeling all right?"

"Just cold and tired."

"You'll miss dinner."

"I'm not hungry."

"Suit yourself," Madame Golinda said, giving Cassie a curious look before heading downstairs.

Wrapping herself in a blanket and lying down fully clothed on the other blanket, Cassie thought over her options. She hated leaving the puppeteers. Yet after coming so far, she couldn't chance being returned to slavery. She could no longer delay. She must leave the puppeteers this very night after everyone was asleep. Until then, she would stay out of sight of the man with one eye.

31
Into the Snow

At bedtime, it was still snowing. Little by little, the ordinary grew quiet as the travelers turned in for the night. It seemed like a long time before the women in the two beds stopped stirring and their breathing became slow and regular. Cassie couldn't settle down and got tangled in the blankets that made up her pallet as she tossed and turned. She was glad she wasn't sleeping with Madame Golinda as she sometimes had to do. Certainly, Peter's mother would have known something was wrong.

Finally, Cassie was sure everyone was asleep. She got up in the dark, secured her scissors and comb in her pocket, and stole silently down the stairs. On the ground floor, she crept toward the front door. In the taproom, three men still lingered at the dying fire, talking. One of them was the man who thought he recognized her. Heart pounding, Cassie tried to listen to what the men were saying.

One man mumbled a question. Another replied, "The Raleigh Tavern." They were talking about Williamsburg. Cassie began to tremble. She inhaled deeply and walked by the door. She didn't look in the direction of the men, but she imagined they turned to see who was about at this time of night. She feared at any moment the man who had recognized her would raise the alarm. Surely, the Blantons had advertised in the *Virginia Gazette,* offering a reward for her capture.

At the front door, she hesitated, her resoluteness momen-
tarily faltering. She hated leaving Peter without a word. She hated
going out into the dark and the storm.

"Hey you, girl," one of the men called to her. "Where are you
going on a night like this?"

Cassie's heart raced. She lifted the latch and fled outside
into the snow. It had stopped snowing, and a cold moon peaked
in and out of the cloudy sky. She looked around frantically for a
place to hide. Finding none, she hurried into the darkness. She
glanced over her shoulder. The man had closed the door and no
one was looking out of the window. She made a dash for the road,
only vaguely discernable in the pale light of the moon.

A wagon had passed sometime after the snow had stopped
and Cassie followed the wheel tracks in the direction of New York.
Without a coat, she began to shiver. Wind whipped her petticoat
and blew snow into her face. It was light and powdery, and drifts
eighteen inches high made walking difficult.

Cassie hadn't gone far before she began to question the
wisdom of her decision. She had heard about people freezing to
death, and she didn't have much experience being outside in the
cold and snow. Still she struggled forward, growing colder and
colder. It wasn't long before she could no longer feel her feet. She
felt the overwhelming urge to sink into the snow, stretch out, and
rest.

The temptation to stop grew and Cassie was about to give in
to it when ahead on the crest of a small hill, she saw a house and
a barn. The thought of the barn with its warm hay and animals
gave her strength to plod on a little further.

Too tired and frozen to think about tomorrow, Cassie reached
the barn, opened the big door a crack, and went inside. Two horses
snorted and stamped their feet. Beside their stalls, a ladder reached
into a hayloft. In the dim moonlight that shone through a dirty
window, she shook snow from her petticoat and her mother's jacket
and then gingerly made her way up the ladder, her frozen feet

feeling like logs. In the loft, she hollowed out a nest for herself in the hay. Taking off her wet shoes, she rubbed her feet until she began to feel sensation in them again. Finally, she covered herself with hay. She shivered and shivered and finally slept.

Just before dawn Cassie awoke, feeling sick. Her throat was sore and her head hurt. But sometime soon, someone from the house would be coming to the barn to feed the horses and she must be gone before then. She shook the hay from her clothes and climbed down the ladder. The wind was still blowing, and drifting snow had covered her tracks from the night before. She hoped by the time someone came to the barn, the snow would again cover her tracks.

32
Amos Heckel

During the night the snow in the wagon tracks had frozen and now Cassie slipped and slid, keeping her balance with great difficulty. The man with the eyepatch might be out looking for her, hoping for a reward. She kept looking behind her and to her relief didn't see anyone on the road. Her thoughts turned to the puppeteers, wondering if they had discovered her departure. She told herself it was better this way, better they never knew who she really was.

The sun came fully up although it seemed to give no warmth. A chill gave Cassie goose bumps. A few minutes later, she was wet with sweat. Each step was an effort and she focused on putting one foot ahead of the other.

Her concentration was broken by the creak of a wagon behind her. Could it be the man with the eyepatch coming after her? She moved off the road, so that the wagon could pass, keeping her head down, not daring to see who was in the wagon. To her alarm, the driver pulled up the horses.

"Want a ride, girlie?" the man asked.

Cassie looked up. It wasn't the man with the eyepatch, but she didn't like the look of the man offering her a ride. He wore a battered cocked hat with greasy hair beneath it and a greatcoat covered with either dog or cat hairs.

The man laughed, showing large yellow teeth. "I won't eat you," he said.

He looked inhuman enough to eat a girl of Cassie's size. Yet her weakness and sickness overcame her judgment. Maybe the man with the eyepatch would be along next. She climbed up into the wagon and sat down. The man called to the horses and they lurched forward.

"Name's Heckel," he said. "Amos Heckel. What's yours?"

Cassie hesitated again. It seemed wrong to tell this man her name.

"Cat got your tongue?"

"Cassandra B-Byrdsong."

"Where're you going, Cassandra B-Byrdsong?" the man said, imitating her stutter.

Cassie didn't want to tell this unkempt man her business. So she said nothing, but her face must have revealed her distress.

"What's the matter, Cassandra? Can't you take a little teasing?"

They rode on in silence for a while. They met another wagon going in the opposite direction. Cassie decided that as soon as the man stopped, she would walk again.

"You're a runaway, aren't you? Why else would you be out on the road without a coat on such a bitter morning after a heavy snow?"

The word *runaway* made her react. "I'm going to New York to find my father. My other folks died."

"So, you're all by yourself." Cassie didn't like Heckel's self-satisfied tone of voice. Too late, she realized she shouldn't have let him know she was by herself.

"I won't b-be as soon as I get to New York." Cassie fought waves of nausea. As sick as she was, she had to get away from this dreadful man. She considered jumping down from the moving wagon, but she would hurt herself if she did.

Time passed slowly and it seemed like a very long time before Heckel pulled up the horses in front of a mill. As soon as the wagon came to a stop, Cassie jumped down onto the icy road.

She scurried away, eager to put as much distance between Amos Heckel and herself as she could.

Heckel called out to a gangly young man who came out of the mill, "Stop that girl! She's a runaway indentured servant!"

Cassie gasped and started to run. The young man charged after her and in a few quick steps, caught her, grabbing her arm. "Do I get a reward?" he called to Heckel.

Cassie struggled, trying to get away, but the young man held on to her tightly. "I'm not a r-r-runaway," she blurted out, realizing that her stutter made her sound like she was lying.

Heckel looked uncomfortable, but he took a coin from his pocket and tossed it to the young man. "Give her to me and get my flour," he said, "and make it snappy." The young man turned her over to Heckel and went into the mill.

Heckel held Cassie with one brawny arm and took a rope from the back of the wagon, with the other. He looped it, put it around her neck, and then tied her hands with it. "This will teach you to run away. And I'll get a fat reward."

The young man returned with a sack of flour that he put into the back of the wagon.

"I'm not a r-r-runaway." Tears streamed down Cassie's face. But neither Heckel nor the young man paid any attention to her plea. "I'm not a r-r-runaway." How could anyone believe her when she couldn't even say the word *runaway* without stuttering?

"Into the wagon," Heckel demanded, motioning to her.

Cassie shook her head, refusing to climb into the wagon. Heckel slapped her face. "Get up there!"

Her face stinging from the blow, she had no choice but to climb into the bed of the wagon with the flour. Heckel fastened the rope about her neck to a ring bolt on the side of the wagon.

He paid the young man for the flour, got into the driver's seat, and flicked the reins. The wagon again bounced forward on the icy road.

Hopelessness engulfed Cassie as she wondered where they were going and what would happen to her. She thought about her worn petticoat, soggy shoes, and stained jacket. She looked like she belonged with Amos Heckel. No one would believe she had met him only an hour ago.

She struggled against the rope that tied her to the wagon, choking with her efforts. "Calm down, Cassandra," he called back to her. "You're going nowhere."

Cassie tried to fight her rising panic. I have to think, she told herself. She shifted her position to try to take the pressure off her neck. As she did so, she felt the cold, hard metal of the scissors in her pocket. Slowly she inched her bound hands inside her petticoat, angling out the scissors. With great difficulty, she began to saw at the rope with one blade of the scissors. At any minute, Heckel might turn and see her. She worked frantically, her heart pounding. The rope frayed and finally she cut through it. Once her hands were free, she removed the noose from around her neck. As she let go of the rope, the ring bolt clanged against the side of the wagon. Heckel turned at the sound and called out to the horses, "Whoa!"

Leaping from the wagon, Cassie ran. She looked over her shoulder and saw he was following her. Unused to ice, Heckel struggled to keep his balance, his arms flailing in every direction. Driven by fear, Cassie sped forward.

33
Widow Bright

Cassie looked over her shoulder again. She was just in time to see Heckel's feet fly out from beneath him. She kept running, her heart pounding. Then she slipped on the ice-sheeted road, and almost went down.

She wanted to leave the treacherous road, but she'd make tracks in the snow. What should she do? To her surprise, she saw that Heckel had gotten up but wasn't following her. He got back into the wagon and was turning it around.

Leaving the road, Cassie ran up a hill, slipping on the snow-covered slope. Her side hurt and her breath came in short gasps. Ahead was a little country meetinghouse with the tombstones in its cemetery half covered with drifts of snow. She reached the meetinghouse, plowing through a high snowdrift to the front door. She lifted the latch and the door opened. She stumbled inside, breathing heavily.

The meetinghouse was very plain, like no church she had ever seen, and cold, the deep cold of an infrequently used building in winter. Four straight-backed benches were the only furnishings in the stark room.

Listening to every sound, Cassie wondered when Heckel would come for her. She collapsed into the corner of one of the straight-backed benches, knowing she was unable to go any farther. She heard raised voices through the heavy door, but she couldn't make out what was being said. She still held her scissors in her hand. Heckel wouldn't capture her without a struggle.

The grating sound of the door latch brought Cassie to her feet. She stepped backward, raising the hand clenching the scissors. Her hand shook as the door opened.

"What are thee doing in this cold place, child?" a gray-haired, stubby woman completely dressed in black asked.

Relief flooded through Cassie. It wasn't Heckel.

"I've sent away an unsavory looking fellow, lurking in front of the meetinghouse. I could tell he was up to no good," the woman said.

Suddenly dizzy, Cassie lowered the scissors and sat down on the nearest bench. She didn't know what to say. She had explained herself so many times to so many different people she had run out of things to say. She started to cry.

The woman came closer, took off her glove, and put her hand on Cassie's forehead. "Just as I thought, thee's ill."

Riding Chair, Colonial Williamsburg
Author Photograph

The woman sat beside her and without hesitation took Cassie into her arms. "There, there, my dear. Thee can tell me about it later. My riding chair is outside. Does thee think thee can walk?"

Cassie nodded. The woman helped her up, out the door, and into her small two-wheeled carriage. "I'm Widow Bright. I come here every day to visit my husband's and son's graves, even in the snow. I wouldn't have gone in the meetinghouse, except I saw thee's footprints and figured something was amiss."

Cassie couldn't think what to say. "I'm sorry for your l-loss," she managed to get out.

Not more than ten minutes later, Widow Bright pulled up in front of a gray stone house nestled into the side of a hill. She helped Cassie down from the carriage and putting an arm around her waist managed to get her into the house. In a sparsely furnished sitting room, a cheerful fire crackled in the fireplace. Widow Bright led her to a chair and pulled a cord that hung near the fireplace. A red-faced serving woman came into the room. "You rang, ma'am?" she asked.

"We have a guest, Maud, a half-frozen, ill, and probably starved, waif. I found her at the meetinghouse. She'll need a bath as soon as the water heats, and lay out one of my shifts for her. She'll need a bowl of your good soup, too."

The servant left, shaking her head. "After thee's warm and fed, then thee can tell me who thou are and what thee was doing at our meetinghouse," Widow Bright said.

Before long, dressed in a clean shift, Cassie climbed into the four poster bed in Widow Bright's guest room. Maud had warmed the bed with a bed warmer and now she covered her with a colorful quilt. Almost instantly, Cassie fell into a feverish sleep.

She lost track of time. She woke and slept, had more soup, and slept again. She coughed and her throat was sore. She was either too hot or too cold. At one point, a doctor visited, opened her eyelid, and looked at her eye. Then he listened to her chest. Cassie heard Widow Bright talking with the doctor and with the woman named Maud, but for the most part, for Cassie, days passed in a blur.

One morning she awoke and looked around. Widow Bright sat in a rocking chair near the fire, knitting. "So thee's decided to live," she said, putting down her knitting and coming to sit in a chair next to Cassie's bed. "We've been very worried about thee."

Cassie's last clear memory was getting into the big bed. "How l-long have I b-been sick?"

"Ten days."

Cassie gasped. "Thank you for caring for me."

"You have given me much to think about. The day I found thee, I was in the depth of despair." Widow Bright sniffled. "My only son fought with the Patriots. He was wounded at Saratoga and we got him home, but he died from his wounds. Soon afterward, my husband died of grief. I thought I was the most miserable of beings. Then I saw thee. Something told me thee had suffered greatly also."

Widow Bright sat quietly for a moment as if lost in thought. "I'm a member of the Society of Friends, most people call us Quakers. We're a plain people, dedicated to serving others and against war and slavery."

Cassie had heard of Quakers. Some lived at Skimino Creek west of Williamsburg. But she didn't know anything about them until she had seen the Quaker man defend the fallen slave in Philadelphia. "I wondered why you talked differently. I talk differently, too."

Quaker Meeting (from an eighteenth-century illustration)

Bowles & Carver, *Old English Cuts and Illustrations* (New York: Dover, 1970), p. 19

"Friends choose to use plain forms of address, most notably *thee* and *thou*. I believe once thee is assured of thee's place in the world and thee's rights as a human being, thee'll gradually conquer thee's stuttering. Can thee tell me about theeself now?" Widow Bright asked.

Cassie looked into the woman's kind, lined face. Warm gray eyes looked back at her from behind thick glasses. Something told her it was probably time for the truth, but she didn't want to return to slavery. She had once believed in the kindness of Mrs. Nichols, only to be heartlessly traded. Widow Bright seemed kind, but could she be trusted? When she found out Cassie wasn't white, would Widow Bright turn her over to the authorities? Would her kindness disappear like last winter's snows?

Widow Bright must have noticed her hesitation. "Let's wait until thee's stronger." The older woman stood, went back to her chair by the fire, and took up her knitting again.

In the days that followed, Cassie slept less, and gradually grew well enough to sit up in bed. The day finally came when she was strong enough to dress. Maud had washed her clothes, and Cassie put on her well-worn shift, petticoat, and her mother's jacket. She still hadn't explained her presence in the meetinghouse to Widow Bright. Now Cassie knew she couldn't put it off any longer.

In the long hours of her recovery, she had debated what to tell Widow Bright. Cassie hadn't purposely deceived the puppeteers, but she had gone along with their assumption she was white. But she wasn't white and she wasn't free. She didn't want to return to Blanton Hall and slavery. At the same time, she didn't want to lie to Widow Bright who had saved her, cared for her, and even called in a doctor on her behalf. Wasn't it time to tell the truth, to accept who she was, even if it meant she would be sent back into slavery?

Cassie made her way with uncertain steps downstairs, holding on to the banister for support. She found Widow Bright in a small sitting room where she sat reading in the light that came in from an east window.

Widow Bright looked up at Cassie, smiled, and closing her book, put it on a nearby table. "It is so good to see thee up and about. Come and sit." Widow Bright indicated the chair near her own. The kind look on her face helped Cassie come to a decision.

The December sun streamed through the window. She sat for a moment, resting from the effort of dressing and coming downstairs. Then she took a deep breath and told Widow Bright everything. Tears rolled down her cheeks when she told Widow Bright about Aunt Ida and Moses, about Zinnia, and the terrible encounter with Amos Heckel. Wiping frantically at her eyes, Cassie looked questioningly at Widow Bright, wondering how she would react. Cassie concluded, "I want to be free. I want to find my father. But I am what I am. I can no longer pretend to be someone I'm not."

34

Charles Goodfellow

Widow Bright shook her head. "Poor, poor child, I'll not send you back to Blanton Hall. You were very sick the day I found you and many days afterwards, and I'm not sure you remember and understood what I told you. I'm a member of the Society of Friends, Quakers to most people, and we don't believe in slavery."

Cassie eyes filled again, but this time her tears were of relief and gratitude. Widow Bright handed her a handkerchief. "Now, now," she said, patting Cassie's arm. "I'd like to help thee find thee's father. I have many contacts in New York among the Society of Friends."

Cassie looked at Widow Bright through her tears. Seeing the compassion in her lined face, Cassie's heart leapt. She dried her eyes. She wanted to hug dear Widow Bright, but she wasn't sure if Quakers hugged. So Cassie reached out and took Widow Bright's small, pudgy hand in hers and squeezed it. "Thank you," Cassie murmured. "Thank you."

Following her confession, Cassie and Widow Bright fell into a comfortable routine. Widow Bright wrote a number of letters on Cassie's behalf. When Widow Bright found out Cassie knew the alphabet and could read a few words, she spent several hours each day working with Cassie on her reading.

Ten days before Christmas, the mail brought a reply. They were just finishing a reading lesson in the sunny sitting room, and Widow Bright was putting away the paper and ink she had used for the lessons. She read the brief letter and then looked up and smiled. "One of the Friends has found a former slave calling himself Charles Goodfellow. We think he's your father. He's a bricklayer and a mason who arrived in New York with Lord Dunmore and subsequently joined the Black Pioneers. He was honorably discharged from the British army after being wounded."

Cassie leapt from her chair, her heart pounding. "How will I know for sure?"

"We'll have to go there and meet him."

"You'll come with me?"

Widow Bright rose from her chair with a smile. "I'll drive my phaeton. We'll go tomorrow."

Cassie was glad the day's lesson was over because she knew she couldn't sit still. To build her strength, Widow Bright had suggested she walk about the house and up and down the stairs to the second floor. Now Cassie's feet were light as she began to retrace the familiar route.

Could this Charles Goodfellow really be her father? Or would this be another disappointment? She passed the clock in the hallway and glanced at the time. How could she wait until tomorrow?

The next morning Cassie was up and dressed soon after it grew light. She went to the kitchen in the back of the house to help Maud prepare breakfast. To her surprise, she found Widow Bright already up and dressed, sitting at the kitchen table drinking a cup of tea. Could it be she was as excited as Cassie about the possibility of finding her father?

"Good morning," Widow Bright said, "I'm glad thee's up. We'll get an early start. Yesterday afternoon, I procured a cloak for thee. It's not new, but it's warm." She took a gray cloak, just about Cassie's size, from where it lay folded on a chair. "It belonged to a daughter of one of the Friends and she's outgrown it. Now it belongs to thee."

Cassie took the warm-looking cloak. "How can I ever thank you, Widow Bright?"

"Thee doesn't need to, my dear. Thee should know by now, helping thee has helped me."

An hour later, fortified with Maud's porridge sweetened with maple syrup, they were on the road to New York. Dressed in the warm cloak and covered with a thick horse blanket, Cassie rode beside Widow Bright. Dirty snow banks lined the road and the phaeton rumbled over the frozen ruts and occasional patches of ice.

Phaeton (from an eighteenth-century illustration)

Bowles & Carver, *Old English Cuts and Illustrations* (New York: Dover, 1970), p. 50

As they traveled closer to New York, Cassie began to doubt that this Charles Goodfellow was indeed her father. Maybe her father was dead or had just disappeared. He had always gone by the name Loatwell, his master's name, in Williamsburg. What would she do if he wasn't her father?

Her somber thoughts lifted a little as they saw the city across the river. They drove to a ferry where a British soldier stood guard. "Halt!" he ordered in a threatening voice.

Cassie spirits plummeted. But Widow Bright calmly took out her pocket and produced a paper that she handed the soldier. He read the paper and brought it to another soldier who stood nearby.

"It's a pass," Widow Bright explained. "The British let us come and go into the city because we are pacifists."

Cassie had not heard the word "pacifist" before, but she assumed it meant peace-loving since the Quakers were against war. Nonetheless, she was confused. "But your son was a Continental soldier, a Patriot," Cassie whispered, as they waited for the soldier to return.

"He went against our beliefs." Widow Bright's voice quavered. "He believed he was fighting for liberty, and to him it was more important than our teachings."

Cassie searched for words of comfort. "Your son was right. Nothing is m-more important than freedom. But the Friends are right too. War is terrible."

Widow Bright's brow furrowed. Before she could respond, the soldier returned to the phaeton, handed back the pass, and motioned them onto the ferry.

On board the ferry, Cassie studied the city she had thought about so often. It didn't appear much different from the other cities she had visited. The difference was that her father might be here.

"We can get down and stand at the railing," Widow Bright said after the ferryman had secured her horse and phaeton. "This is the Hudson River, and New York is on an island, Manhattan Island."

Cassie stood with Widow Bright as the ferry got under way and little by little, New York grew closer. Seagulls squawked and swirled overhead, and the chilly winter sun glittered on the water. Cassie's thoughts turned to the man she hadn't seen for six years. She wondered if they would recognize each other. She had put on her mother's jacket. But she wasn't sure he would remember it. If he did remember it and recognize her, would he be glad to see her? And could she stay with him?

35
Manda and Anthony

The ferry eased into the wharf on Manhattan Island. The pungent smell of rotting fish filled the air. Two mangy tomcats prowled the pier near where workmen were unloading a barge. Widow Bright drove the phaeton off the ferry, and Cassie climbed in beside her.

They drove on a short distance. "I need to ask directions," Widow Bright said, pulling up on the reins near a young man who was selling newspapers.

"Am I headed in the direction of Broadway?" she asked.

"Yes, ma'am," the young man said. "Go to the corner and turn, go over two blocks and you'll be on Broadway."

Thanking the man, Widow Bright clucked to the horse, and they were on their way again. A number of people were on the streets, and Cassie found herself, as she had at Yorktown, searching each face for her father.

They had been on Broadway for about ten minutes when Widow Bright stopped in front of a construction site. She smiled at Cassie and gave her a reassuring pat. "This is surely the place. Let's see if we can find thee's father's employer. He knows we're coming, so there should be no problem."

They got down from the carriage. "Mr. Putnam?" Widow Bright asked the first workman they saw, a huge man carrying a beam on his shoulder.

"He's in that building," the man said, pointing to a temporary-looking structure.

Widow Bright knocked on the door. "Come in," someone said.

They entered the unpainted building. A balding man wearing glasses sat at a high desk, writing with a quill. He stood when he saw Widow Bright. "Elias Putnam, at your service," he said, bowing formally from the waist. "You must be Widow Bright. I've been informed of the purpose of your visit."

In her nervousness, Cassie barely followed the exchange of pleasantries between Mr. Putman and Widow Bright. Mr. Putnam showed them into an adjoining room, bare except for a table on which there were several drawings and two chairs. "If you'll wait here, I'll send someone for Goodfellow. Good day, ma'am," he said, taking his leave with another bow.

Minutes passed in the cold room. Cassie anxiously paced from the door to the table. What if the man was her father, but he didn't recognize her? Didn't claim her as his daughter?

Finally, the door opened. A tall, muscular man, noticeably limping, came in and stood for a moment in the doorway. She looked searchingly at him for a second. He returned her gaze and then his face lit up, dispelling all of her doubts.

"Cassie, my own Cassie," he said, his voice choking. He knelt and opened his arms. She rushed into them, safe at last in his strong embrace. "Let me look at you," her father said.

She self-consciously withdrew from his embrace. She glanced at Widow Bright who was smiling.

"Thee will have much to talk over," Mrs. Bright said. "I'll wait in the phaeton."

"Tell me everything," her father said, sitting down and grasping both of Cassie's small hands in his large, work-worn ones.

Cassie told her father all she had been through to get to this day, tears springing in her eyes when she told him about Aunt Ida and Moses. However, she brushed them away. Her father's powerful presence was so wonderful she didn't want to ruin their meeting with sad tales of her last months.

Cassie's father studied her face. "You favor your mother right much. I loved her more than my life."

Cassie could wait no longer to ask the question foremost in her mind. "Now that I've found you again, can I stay with you?"

Her father smiled. "Of course, I want you to stay with me."

"Are you sure?"

"I've lost you once. I never intend to lose you again."

Tears of joy welled in Cassie's eyes. She smiled at him. "Oh, Father, there's nothing I want more."

Like a cloud that suddenly crosses the sun, a frightening thought came to her mind. She struggled to cast it aside, but she couldn't. "What will happen to us if the Patriots win the war? Will we be sent back to slavery?"

Her father's face grew serious. "The British have promised they won't abandon us. I served them five years."

"Do you believe them? They abandoned me and lots of others at Yorktown."

"I don't know what choice we've got, Cassie."

"I never want to go back to being a slave. I've liked being free too much."

"I love being free, too, Cassie, and just as I don't intend to be separated from you again, I don't intend to be a slave again."

Her father paused as if carefully weighing what he was going to say next. "There's one thing you should know right away. I've remarried and you have a little brother."

It had never occurred to Cassie her father might have remarried, and she was afraid her face revealed her disappointment. After a moment, she managed to say, "I guess I never really believed I'd find you. I just didn't have anyone else."

"Well, you do now. You have not only me, but a whole family."

Cassie heard a light rap on the door. Her father went to the door. "Please come in, Widow Bright."

"It's time I was heading back to New Jersey," Widow Bright said.

"I don't know how Cassie and I can ever repay you," Charles Goodfellow said.

"Seeing the looks on thee's faces was payment enough," Widow Bright said. "There are some things still unsettled. Would it be possible for thee, Cassie, and thee's family to meet me here Saturday at five P.M.?"

Cassie's father didn't hesitate. "Of course, we are eternally in your debt."

"By then I hope to have information about thee's Mrs. Byrdsong, Cassie. I'll see thee on Saturday."

Widow Bright turned to go, but Cassie caught up with her. "Thank you for everything," she said, giving the widow the hug she had kept in her heart for so many days.

Widow Bright didn't appear flustered at all. She hugged Cassie back. "I'll see you Saturday."

Cassie and her father watched Widow Bright drive away. Father cleared his throat. "Mr. Putnam has given me leave to take you home and then come back. I'll introduce you to your stepmother and brother."

They made their way along crowded city streets near British army barracks. As they walked along side by side, her father reached out and took Cassie's hand in his own. Once again, after so many years, the familiar security of the calloused, big hand made her heart leap. She was home at last.

They came to a neat, white cottage, tucked in halfway behind a bigger building and her father slowed. Cassie was glad that she was meeting her stepmother right away. She hoped her stepmother would like and accept her.

Her father opened the door into a small sitting room containing a worn sofa and two straight-back chairs. "Manda, we're home," he said as if he and Cassie had just gone for a walk.

A tall, comely, brown-skinned woman came from the back room. She wiped her hands on the apron she was wearing. "Hello, Cassie," she said smiling, deep dimples showing in each cheek.

"When the Quaker man contacted Charles, I was hoping the run-away girl was really you."

"Hello," Cassie said, wondering what she should call her stepmother.

"You can call me Manda. I'm so happy you're here. I'm baking a pie in your honor."

Cassie's father motioned toward the door. "I have to be getting back. I'll see you both later." He stooped and hugged Cassie and then gave Manda a peck on the cheek.

Cassie watched him disappear out the door. She stood uneasily in the hallway. She hardly knew her father, and now she was left alone with a stranger. Just then, a small boy, the same color as his mother, toddled into the room.

"This is Anthony," Manda said. "Anthony, say hello to Cassie."

Anthony hid behind his mother's skirt. He peered around it to smile shyly at Cassie, showing dimples like his mother's. "Hello, Anthony," Cassie said, charmed by her new brother.

Manda took charge. "Come into the kitchen. We'll finish up the pie."

The kitchen was a narrow room at the back of the cottage with exposed beams and a large fireplace. Anthony still hid in his mother's skirt. "Have a seat and make yourself comfortable."

Cassie sat at the unpainted kitchen table, glancing around. A shelf displayed blue and white china plates, and an iron kettle simmered in the fieldstone fireplace, filling the room with the pleasant smells of cooking chicken.

At the table, Manda finished rolling out the pie dough, put it into a pan, and then filled the pan with apples, sugar, and butter. Cassie watched her work, wondering if she would ever fit into her new family.

Manda put the pie into the oven on the side of the fireplace. "Your father's special. I knew the first day I met him that he was the one for me." She sat beside Cassie.

Cassie was curious about Manda. "Are you an escaped slave, too?"

"No, my family has lived in New York for as long as anyone can remember. Tell me how you got all the way from Virginia to New York."

Cassie found herself wishing that Manda had known slavery. Cassie knew it was wrong to think that way, but Manda would never really understand what Cassie and her father had been through. She told her story to Manda and as Cassie talked, Anthony edged closer and closer to her. Finally, he climbed into her lap. Anthony was sitting in her lap when her father returned from work.

As the next days passed, like Anthony, little by little Cassie overcame her shyness around her new family. Her father's real pleasure with her presence went a long way to dispel her unease.

Friday evening, Cassie got up courage and asked her father, "There was something Aunt Ida didn't tell me that last night in Williamsburg. She said what I d-didn't know couldn't hurt me. Do you know what it m-might have been?"

Cassie's father thought for a moment. "I guess you're old enough now and we're far enough from Williamsburg that it won't hurt you." He paused before going on. "You may have wondered why I have a new name. I grew to hate the name Loatwell. Josiah Loatwell, my master, was also my father, your grandfather."

Cassie remembered seeing Josiah Loatwell, an elderly white gentleman, on the street in Williamsburg. She wouldn't have noticed him, except Moses had told her that Loatwell was her father's master. She didn't know how to feel about this revelation. But the hurt look on her father's face made her realize the enormity of his pain.

Her white grandfather helped to explain how Cassie could pass for white. It explained much else too. She had never wondered why Josiah Loatwell had sent her father to the Bray school in Williamsburg to learn to read and write and later apprenticed him to a bricklayer. But it was clear to her now that Loatwell hadn't cared enough about her father, his son, to set him free, but had wanted him educated. If anyone guessed her father's parentage, his accomplishments would be a credit to his Loatwell blood.

"How could your father hold his own son in slavery and never see his granddaughter? What sort of a man could do this?" Cassie asked. "He isn't someone I want to know. Will he want you b-back?"

"Probably. But, I don't intend to give up my freedom or yours." Father shook his head sadly and his face seemed to close. Cassie decided not to ask him any more questions right now, but she wondered what threat this Josiah Loatwell was to her and her father. Yet whatever happened, she would no longer have to face it alone.

36
At the Theater Royal

Saturday came and Cassie, her father, Manda, and Anthony went to the construction site. It was after five o'clock when Widow Bright arrived. "I've had news about your Mrs. Byrdsong," Widow Bright said to Cassie after meeting everyone. "She and her family are prisoners of war in Charlottesville, Virginia. They'll be exchanged sometime soon."

"I'm so glad they're safe," Cassie said. "I've told Father and Manda how kind Mrs. Byrdsong was to me at Yorktown."

"Yes, that's wonderful news." Widow Bright smiled and then her face grew somber. "Unfortunately, I found out nothing about your friend Zinnia, except that she wasn't returned to Blanton Hall."

Cassie's relief over Mrs. Byrdsong's safety was overshadowed by her memories of Zinnia being forced out of Yorktown. Cassie hoped Zinnia was safe somewhere and free.

"But that's not the reason I've asked to meet you here," Widow Bright continued. "I have a special treat." Mrs. Bright gave Cassie a handbill.

Cassie recognized it immediately. She had seen similar handbills when she was with the puppeteers. It was an advertisement for Madame Golinda's Punch and Joan Show.

"I've gotten tickets for the six-o'clock show. We'll have to hurry. They're performing at the Theater Royal on John Street."

Cassie's heart fell. Widow Bright obviously thought she was doing her yet another favor. She wanted to see Peter, but now in the company of her family, he would realize she wasn't white. He had believed in her, trusted her, and she had abandoned the puppeteers just as the British had abandoned her. She didn't know what she would say to him.

"I look forward to personally thanking the puppeteers for taking Cassie in," Father said. "Again, Widow Bright, we are eternally in your debt."

"I'll take the children with me in the phaeton. We'll go slowly so you and Mistress Goodfellow can follow along behind."

In the phaeton with Anthony on her lap, Cassie's doubts returned. She longed to see Peter again, to thank him for all he had done for her. But she feared he would hate her. She remembered his remark about Negroes lying and cheating. Surely he would be angry with her for deceiving him.

As they neared the theater, Cassie recognized Jacko outside, playing his fiddle to attract customers. Peter and Madame Golinda were nowhere in sight. Jacko put down his fiddle and began his sales pitch. She knew by heart the words he said. He seemed to look right at her, but if he recognized her, he gave no sign. Her thoughts flew back to her time with the puppeteers. She had enjoyed the privileges that went with being white, but she had always felt she was not herself. Just as she assumed different roles in the puppet theater, she had only been playing a role as Cassandra Byrdsong.

Was there some way she could avoid meeting the puppeteers? No, Widow Bright had planned this reunion, and Jacko had seen her. Reluctantly, Cassie followed Widow Bright and her family into the theater.

The puppet show began. As before, Cassie soon became caught up in the pleasure of the performance and the reaction of the crowd. Anthony squealed with delight when the spotted dog bit Punch's big nose.

The crowd erupted into cheers and was clapping as the final act finished. Cassie wished she could run away and not have to

Punch getting his nose bitten
(from a George Cruikshank illustration)

*The Tragical Comedy or Comical Tragedy of Punch and
Judy* (Cambridge: Washburn and Thomas, 1925)

face Peter. But she was through running. There was no way she could avoid meeting him.

The crowd dispersed and Jacko went behind the stage. She imagined him telling Madame Golinda and Peter about her. A minute later, Peter rushed from backstage and looked around eagerly until he spotted Cassie. He came over to her, a broad smile on his face.

"Hello, Peter," Cassie said, smiling at him in spite of her dread. She turned to the others. "This is Widow B-Bright who has been wonderful to me and my father, Charles Goodfellow, his wife M-Manda, and my little brother Anthony."

Peter seemed taken aback, confused. He bowed politely but he was unable to disguise his shock that she wasn't white. She looked white and had passed for white, but clearly her father, her stepmother, and her brother were people of color.

Cassie's father acknowledged Peter's bow with one of his own. "Pleased to make your acquaintance," he said. "My daughter told me you gave her tremendous help and encouragement."

"It was our pleasure," Peter said politely.

Cassie's words came in a rush. "I'm so sorry that I deceived you, Peter. And I didn't want to run out on you without a word of explanation. I was afraid, afraid the one-eyed man recognized me and would give me away. I didn't want to go b-back to b-being a slave."

Peter usually so glib said nothing. Madame Golinda and Jacko joined them. Cassie introduced her family and Widow Bright.

"Cassandra, we were very worried about you," Madame Golinda said. "You chose the worst night of the year to go looking for your father. I guessed you were running away from someone or something. And since I always play my cards close to my chest, I respected your right to do so."

Cassie looked gratefully at Madame Golinda, appreciating her fully for the first time. She might be blunt and businesslike, but she was a good person. She wasn't much for hugs, but Peter was lucky to have her for a mother. If he had been blind to the possibility Cassie was an escaped slave, Madame Golinda had not been.

"We like our freedom so much we don't even stay in one place. We can understand you wanting to be free," Jacko said, pulling thoughtfully on one side of his mustache.

"Won't you come back and help us with our New York performances?" Madame Golinda said, glancing down at her gnarled hands. "It would be a favor to me."

Widow Bright spoke up, "You can talk all this over later. I've booked the private parlor at The Thistle and Crown Tavern. It's not far from here. I'd like you all to be my guests for a meal."

Everyone seemed to speak at once agreeing to her proposal. A moment later, they were all heading in the direction of the nearby tavern. Cassie walked side by side with Peter. "I'm sorry, Peter," she said again.

Peter smiled a bit sadly. "I'm just happy you're safe. I never thought we'd keep you forever. I knew you'd leave if, or when, you found your father. You did surprise and worry us leaving as you did."

"You must know I loved being a puppeteer."

Peter was quiet for moment. "I have a confession. I hoped you wouldn't find your father. I never had a clue you were . . . running away. You were just Cassandra, Cassie, someone my age whose company I enjoyed, my friend."

Cassie returned his smile. "Oh Peter, I'm so glad you don't hate me."

Peter looked at her for a long moment and then his face crinkled into his familiar grin. "I hope you can work with us, but whatever you do, I want you to know I could never, ever hate you."

Author's Note

Cassie and the other main characters in *Between the Lines* are fictional. However, the events in the story are true and based on soldiers' diaries, journals, correspondence, and other historical records.

On November 15, 1775, John Murray, Earl of Dunmore, Royal Governor of Virginia, faced with colonial rebellion, issued a proclamation offering freedom to any slaves who would join the British. In the Revolutionary War (1776–1783) that followed, no one knows how many runaways joined the British. The fate of the runaway slaves was often grim, none grimmer than the former slaves who were abandoned at Yorktown.

Most runaways did not serve as soldiers. Like Cassie in our story, they served in auxiliary capacities: women working as cooks, maids, and laundresses, men as foragers or laborers. At Yorktown, former slaves helped to construct the fortifications. The estimates of the number of runaways at Yorktown range from 3,000 to 7,000. These former slaves had no tents or blankets and many became ill. Smallpox was rampant and approximately 60 percent of the runaways caught the often fatal disease. In hopes of infecting the Continental army and their allies, the British commander, General Cornwallis, forced these ill former slaves out of Yorktown.

Cornwallis' attempt at biological warfare did not succeed because General George Washington had ordered the secret inoculation of his army against smallpox in 1777. Thomas Jefferson estimated that of the 30,000 slaves that joined the British during the Revolutionary War, 27,000 died of smallpox and camp fever.

Modern historians have estimated the total number of slaves who escaped to the British was between 80,000 and 100,000. A recent study by Cassandra Pybus in the *William and Mary Quarterly* puts the number between 20,000 and 25,000.

When the British food supplies ran low at Yorktown, the British cast out the remaining runaways, about 2,000 former slaves, between the lines in the no-man's land separating the armies. Most of the slaves who survived the battle and illness were recaptured and returned to slavery.

One of the unknowable facts of history is how many African Americans have passed as white. In Colonial America a person was either white or Negro. No middle ground was recognized. However, as in the case of the heroine of our story, it wasn't always easy to tell a person's race by their skin color and appearance.

Puppeteers traveled about the countryside in the eighteenth century, stopping at the major population centers to perform. The most popular shows were dramatizations of the adventures of Punch and Joan. Hand puppets of various designs and moveable theaters could be used for informal presentations on the street. Wire puppet performances were usually in theaters or in large rooms in a tavern.

From eighteenth-century records, we know George Washington paid 11 shillings sixpence in November 1776 to see a puppet show. And while Thomas Jefferson was a student at the College of William and Mary in Williamsburg, he attended a puppet show. The archives at Colonial Williamsburg mention a young slave girl, a few years older than Cassie, who ran off with a group of traveling players.

The Quakers were among the few religious groups who questioned the morality of slavery. They formed the first American anti-slavery society in 1775. In 1780, the year before this story takes place, Pennsylvania, the center of Quakerism in the colonies, had passed an Act for the Gradual Abolition of Slavery.

My treatment of Cassie's stuttering comes from personal experience and from years of interest in, and reading about the problem. It is not uncommon for people who stutter to sing or act without stuttering. Many people gradually overcome the handicap, as I did, and Cassie is on her way to doing so by the end of the book. Stress is one thing that makes stuttering worse.

For the most part, historians can only guess at how slaves spoke in the eighteenth century. Certainly, slaves in different occupations spoke differently. However, a number of first-hand accounts from the period note what good English was spoken by the slaves in Williamsburg.

Cassie's story doesn't end with her arrival in New York at Christmas, 1781. Her position will become tenuous when the British make peace with the Patriots and the British again have to decide what to do with the runaways who helped them during the war.

Glossary

apprentice. A young person taken on by a master craftsman for training. Usually, the apprenticeship lasted seven years.

assembly. A ceremony with the music of the fifes and drums at which the commanding officer inspected the troops and gave the orders of the day.

Black Pioneers and Guards. The most famous Black **Loyalist** military unit, founded in 1776. The Pioneers' main duty was to build fortifications. They were not allowed to fight as regular soldiers and they were divided into companies that were assigned to various military units.

breeches. Knee-length pants.

cocked hat. A hat turned up on three sides. Today we call hats worn during the American Revolution tricorn hats.

Continental army. This was the army raised by the Continental Congress in 1775 to fight the British in the **Revolutionary War**. These were trained soldiers in contrast to the militia that consisted of ordinary citizens.

Cornwallis, Charles (1738–1805). A British general during the **Revolutionary War**. He was arguably the most famous British general of his day. His great success in the Carolina Campaign was followed by defeat at the Battle of Yorktown in 1781. Although the war went on for two more years, the defeat of Cornwallis for all practical purposes ended the British effort to reestablish their authority over the new nation.

Dunmore's Proclamation. James Murray, Earl of Dunmore and Royal Governor of Virginia, issued a proclamation on November 15, 1775, when confronted with rebellion in Virginia. The document offered freedom to runaway slaves and indentured servants who joined the British.

Egyptians. A Scots name for Gypsies. Gypsies in Scotland were ancient traveling people unrelated to the Romany, the group most often designated as **Gypsies.**

greatcoat. A man's overcoat.

Gypsies. Nomadic peoples often used to refer to the Romany people, a group that migrated into Europe from Northern India in the fourteenth century. In seventeenth and eighteenth century Scotland, it was illegal to be a vagabond, and magistrates transported beggars and Gypsies to North America. The term came to be used to designate anyone who moved from place to place.

handbills. A printed advertisement, passed out by hand.

highboy. A tall chest of drawers, sometimes in two sections. Chippendale was a style of eighteenth-century furniture with flowing, graceful lines.

high roll. An eighteenth-century woman's hairstyle in which the hair was piled high on the head. In order to get the desired height, hair pieces made of horse hair, goat hair, and human hair were employed. Sometimes padding was also put into the hairdo for added height.

indentured servants. An indenture is an agreement. Many people came to America in colonial times by agreeing to work for a number of years without pay in return for their passage. They were called indentured servants.

Indian corn. A name the British called native-American corn since it was different from the grains they knew in England. When it is dried, it is hard and must be ground into cornmeal to be edible.

livery. An identifying uniform worn by servants of wealthy landowners.

louvers. Slatted openings, usually for ventilation or cooling.

Loyalists. During the **Revolutionary War** the Americans who supported the British rather than the Continental Congress were called Loyalists or **Tories**.

millinery shop. In the eighteenth century, a millinery shop was a store where cloth and fashionable accessories were sold. Tailors made the cloth, imported from Europe, into clothes. In the twentieth century, a millinery shop sold women's hats.

mobcap. A frilly hat worn by women in the eighteenth century.

necessary. A latrine or outhouse.

ordinary. An inn or tavern where meals were served.

pacifists. Lovers of peace; pacifists will not fight in wars.

pallet. A temporary bed on the floor for a child. It was usually made of blankets and quilts.

Patriots. People who supported the Continental Congress and independence from Great Britain during the **Revolutionary War**.

petticoat. An eighteenth-century word for a skirt.

phaeton. A small, light, horse-drawn carriage.

pocket. An eighteenth-century purse or pouch, made of cloth and worn under women's clothes. Usually, the pocket was tied around the waist with linen strips. **Petticoats** had slits in the side so that the purse would be accessible.

Punch and Joan. Popular eighteenth-century puppets. Today we know the same puppets as Punch and Judy.

Quakers. Members of the **Society of Friends**. A religious group founded in England in the seventeenth century. The Quakers refused to worship in established churches, bear arms, and take oaths. They were opposed to slavery. The name Quakers comes from an admonition from an early leader that they should tremble before God's word.

reveille. A ceremony at sunrise conducted by the fifes and drums to awaken the army.

Revolutionary War (1776–1783). The thirteen British colonies in America declared their independence from Great Britain on July 4, 1776. In the long war that followed, **Patriots** under the leadership of General George Washington fought against the British armies sent to subdue them. Sometimes called the **War of Independence**.

riding crop. A small whip used on horses.

rheumatism. A popular name for arthritis.

run. Creeks in Virginia are sometimes called runs.

Saratoga. Decisive victory for the **Continental army** on October 17, 1777. This battle influenced France to become an ally of the struggling new nation.

shift. A woman's undergarment worn in the eighteenth century. It was shaped like a man's shirt, only longer.

slave patrols. In 1727 Virginia law required communities to provide an armed group of white men to protect them against possible slave rebellions. Slave patrols searched slave quarters, dispersed slave gatherings, and patrolled the roads. Any slave on the road must show a pass from his or her master.

Society of Friends. A religious group founded in England in the seventeenth century. The Friends refused to worship in established churches, bear arms, and take oaths. They were opposed to slavery. The name **Quakers** comes from an admonition from an early leader that they should tremble before God's word.

stays. A strip of whalebone, ivory, or other material used to stiffen a corset.

sterling. British currency at the time of the Revolutionary War was called pounds sterling or sometimes referred to only as sterling.

stocks. A devise used in Colonial times for punishment. It was composed of heavy wooden timbers used to confine the ankles or the neck and wrists of wrongdoers.

tattoo. A ceremony with music of the fifes and drums in which soldiers were rousted out of the taverns and returned to their tents for the night.

Tory. Another name for the **Loyalists** who favored the continuance of British rule during the **Revolutionary War.**

tow sack. A bag made of coarse woven flax or hemp.

Trooping the Colors. A display of unit flags during a military ceremony.

trundle bed. A low bed that can be stored under another bed.

War of Independence (1776–1783). The thirteen British colonies in America declared their independence from Great Britain on July 4, 1776. In the long war that followed, **Patriots** under the leadership of General George Washington fought against the British armies sent to subdue them. Sometimes called the **Revolutionary War**.

wench. A word often used to describe a servant girl or young woman.

Yorktown. A small Virginia port on the York River and the site of the last major battle of the **Revolutionary War.** The **Continental army** under General George Washington and our French allies defeated **Lord Cornwallis** who surrendered his army to the Americans on October 19, 1781.

Lesson Plans

A. OBJECTIVES

1. To appreciate the timeless social problems of adolescent transition.
2. To learn the geography of the American Revolution, especially as it relates to the Battle of Yorktown and the British in New York City.
3. To understand the issues that separated the Patriots and the Loyalists during the American Revolution with special emphasis on the differing view of slavery.
4. To understand cultural and social problems of the time.
5. To learn words, and the usage of literary devices such as simile and metaphor.
6. To solve problems: A story is a puzzle; the main character has a problem.
7. To understand the past and the passing of time.
8. To gain information.
9. For enjoyment.

B. BACKGROUND, BEFORE READING THE BOOK

1. Introduce the Revolutionary War.

   Explain the difference between a civil war and an international war, noting how the Revolutionary War was both; make comparisons to current events.

2. Fix the Revolutionary War in time.

   Use relative markers such as the time of their great-great-great-grandfathers; a time before airplanes and automobiles; before phones; a time of transportation by horse power; compare the

172

size of cities then and now, national population, then and now. Review the notations for years and centuries.

3. Discuss how the Revolutionary War was a civil war. Give an overview of the early years of the war.

   Emphasize upstart rebels versus people loyal to the king and England; Review the Patriots' dissatisfaction with being ruled from England, the Declaration of Independence, General Washington, the Battle of Saratoga, Valley Forge, and the reasons why the Patriots and British had different views on slavery.

4. Discuss the stress of war.

   Describe the siege warfare and the problems facing African Americans during the war; the uncertainty of loyalty during the war.

5. Explain the separate roles of men and women, boys and girls, at the time of the war.

C. QUESTIONS FOR DISCUSSION

1. The author put a glossary at the back of the book. What is a glossary and how is it different from a dictionary?

2. The pictures in the book are either historical pictures or taken by the author. Why did the author go to the trouble to search out or to take photographs?

3. Where is Cassie's father during the story? Why was he not in Williamsburg?

4. Have you seen any of the places mentioned in the book? The gun shop at Colonial Williamsburg, the battlefield at Yorktown, a Quaker meetinghouse?

5. Discuss the material at the back of the book for planning a trip. Why do we preserve historic sites?

6. What is the problem or conflict of the book? What does Cassie want?

7. Why did the British offer freedom to escaped slaves during the American Revolution?

8. Does Cassie have any mentors in the book? How do the mentors help Cassie survive in the encampment at Yorktown,

adjust to life with the puppeteers, and find her father? Are any teachers, coaches, or ministers your mentor?

9. Books often have a back story. Does *Between the Lines* have a back story, if so what is it?

10. Why is it important that Cassie learned to dress hair?

11. What two meanings does the title *Between the Lines* have?

12. Cassie stutters. Give examples of how this affects her life. What steps does she take to overcome her stuttering?

13. How is the relationship between Cassie and Peter complicated in the book? Why is Cassie afraid that Peter will hate her?

14. An important theme in *Between the Lines* is Cassie's accepting her identity. Why is it so difficult for her to do that? What circumstances allow her to be herself and tell the truth?

15. In two places in the book Quakers appear. Why was this important?

D. LANGUAGE ARTS

1. Writers often foreshadow events in a novel. What is foreshadowing? Is there any foreshadowing in *Between the Lines*?

2. Writers are problem solvers. How could a young slave girl escape from her owners and find her way from Virginia to New York?

3. Writers create characters. What things reveal Cassie's personality? Zinnia's? Adrianna's? Mrs. Byrdsong's? Madame Golinda's? Widow Bright's?

4. What is in a name? How do the names in the story contribute to the story?

5. Writers like to play with words by using similes and/or metaphors. These are comparisons or implied comparisons. Find some in the novel.

E. THINGS TO KNOW

Battle of Yorktown, General Charles Cornwallis

Dunmore Proclamation

Loyalists versus Patriots, Tories versus Colonists

Status of New York City during the Revolution
Time-line progression of events during the Revolution
Revolutionary War
Role of the Quakers
War of Independence
Williamsburg

F. VOCABULARY

bereft	doorjam	outlandishly
blanched	fickleness	pacifist
breeches	forlornly	profuse
broadcloth	glib	revelation
capital	handbills	sanctuary
capitol	intermittently	spindly
confidence	mahogany	stall
crestfallen	midwife	tread
demeaning	millstone	

G. JUST FOR FUN

1. In the book we really don't learn what happens to Cassie at the end of the war. Fill in the gap with an additional chapter.
2. Write this story from the point of view of Adrianna. What does she think of the war? Slaves?
3. Draw a picture of a person or a scene in the book.
4. Write a poem expressing the slaves' desire for freedom at the time of this story.

H. Historical Document Excerpt (November 7, 1775) Dunmore Proclamation

And I do hereby further declare all indentured Servants, Negroes, or others, (appertaining to Rebels,) free that are able and willing to bear Arms, they joining His Majesty's Troops as soon as may be, for the more speedily reducing this Colony to a proper Sense of their Duty, to His Majesty's Crown and Dignity. I do further order, and require, all His Majesty's Leige Subjects, to retain their Quitrents, or any other Taxes due or that may become due, in their own Custody, till such Time as Peace may be again restored to this at present most unhappy Country, or demanded of them for their former salutary Purposes, by Officers properly authorized to receive the same.

GIVEN under my Hand on board the Ship WILLIAM, off Norfolk, the 7th day of November, in the SIXTEENTH Year of His Majesty's Reign.

DUNMORE.

For an original copy of the document see:

Proclamation of John Murray, Earl of Dunmore, Tracy W. McGregor Library of American History, Special Collections, University of Virginia Library.

Questions:

1. Are documents facts? What is the difference between a document and a textbook discussion of the document?

2. Why did Lord Dunmore issue this document?

3. Why was this document issued in 1775?

4. Why do you suppose the document mentions slaves in one sentence and taxes in the next?

I. REVIEW

After completing your discussion of the book, ask children again what they know about the Revolutionary War. You'll be surprised at how much they have learned.

To Plan a Visit

Colonial Williamsburg, Williamsburg, Virginia
More than eighty buildings in historic Colonial Williamsburg are original to the eighteenth century. For more information, contact: "May I Help You" Desk, Colonial Williamsburg Foundation, Williamsburg, Virginia 23185; phone (757) 220-7644, (800) 447-8679; Internet: http://www.history.org

Yorktown National Historic Park, Yorktown, Virginia
The site of the battle of Yorktown is preserved here along with information relating to the battle and the American Revolution. For more information, contact: Yorktown National Historic Park, P.O. Box 210, Yorktown, Virginia 23690; phone: (757) 898-2410. Internet: http://www.nps.gov/col/

Yorktown Victory Center, Yorktown, Virginia
This museum contains much information on the Revolutionary War, the life of the Continental soldiers, and the Yorktown campaign. For more information, contact: Yorktown Victory Center, P.O. Box 1607, Williamsburg, Virginia 23178; phone (757) 253-4823; (800) 456-5563.

Resources

Frey, Sylvia. *Water from the Rock*. Princeton: University Press, 1991. Contains valuable material about the Black Loyalists at Yorktown.

Haislip, Phyllis Hall. *Marching in Time*. Richmond: Dietz Press, 2003. My non-fiction history of fifing and drumming with particular emphasis on Williamsburg and the American Revolution.

Lepore, Jill. "Goodbye Columbus," *The New Yorker* (May 8, 2006), pp. 74–78. An excellent survey of the literature relating to the fate of Black Loyalists during the Revolutionary War.

Martin, Joseph Plumb. *The Diary of Joseph Plumb Martin: A Revolutionary War Soldier*. New York: Benchmark Books, 2001. A firsthand account for kids of the life of a private soldier during the American Revolution.

Feel free to contact the author: phyllis.haislip@gmail.com

Check out the author's website: http://phyllishaislip.com

Of special interest to teachers is the Colonial Williamsburg website: http://history.org/teach for an e-newsletter and free lesson plans for Colonial history.

The Author

Phyllis Hall Haislip has a Ph.D. in history and has spent more than 20 years as a college history teacher. She has always loved history because she loves stories, and history has the word "story" in it. She enjoyed teaching college history, but not as much as she has enjoyed writing for kids. She loves meeting readers—and even gets hugs!

Her first book for kids, *Lottie's Courage*, won the Beacon of Freedom Award. It was very special since kids chose the winner. A children's theater group, Limelight Talent, chose another of the author's books, *Lili's Gift,* for a series of skits. What a thrill to see real children bring her characters to life. As a writer she gets attached to her characters. In fact, they become like her children. She's hesitant to send them out into the world, but it is a joy when readers like them as much as she does.

This is Haislip's fifth book published by White Mane Kids and she also has an e-book called *The Time Magus*. Since her readers grow up, she's been working on an adult novel, for three years, about a twelfth-century wonder woman, Ermengarde, Viscountess of Narbonne.

When she's not writing or visiting schools, Haislip goes on long hikes, carrying a 20-pound backpack on a medieval pilgrimage route in France and Spain.

WHITE MANE PUBLISHING CO., INC.

To Request a Catalog Please Write to:
WHITE MANE PUBLISHING COMPANY, INC.
P.O. Box 708 • Shippensburg, PA 17257
e mail: marketing@whitemane.com
Our Catalog is also available online
www.whitemane.com

CPSIA information can be obtained at www.ICGtesting.com
Printed in the USA
BVOW030128200312

285479BV00005B/4/P